"Where's the bedroom?" Kyle asked

"First door on the right..." Before Theresa could finish her sentence, he'd swept her up in his arms and carried her down the hall.

She braced herself for a rough landing on the bed, but he managed to lay her down gently. His torso pressed into her, a solid weight that thrilled her. For an average-size guy, he was strong. Everywhere she touched, she met hard muscle. The feel of him turned her on so much that her body wasn't paying attention to her mind anymore. She'd been reduced to this all-consuming need.

And the only thing that could take that need away was him.

He moved away suddenly, and without his warmth she felt cold. "What are you doing?" she asked.

Kyle paused, his hand on the snap to his jeans. "I thought you might be tired of being the only one naked."

Dear Reader,

As soon as Theresa Jacobs sauntered onto the pages of *Good, Bad...Better*, Blaze #168, I knew I would have to tell her story in a book of her own. And here it is. *Do Me Right* was an absolute pleasure to write, as I couldn't wait to find out what would happen with Theresa and her hero.

A woman as strong as Theresa demanded an equally strong man. Kyle Cameron had the right combination of cowboy charm and masculine determination to crack her tough exterior and find the tender woman within.

This book also gave me another chance to revisit one of my favorite cities in the world, Austin, Texas. I spent many happy years there and it was nice to remember them.

I hope you enjoy *Do Me Right*. I love to hear from readers. Visit my Web site at www.CindiMyers.com to find out more about what I'm up to. E-mail me at Cindi@cindimyers.com or write me at P.O. Box 991, Bailey, CO 80421.

Happy reading,

Cindi Myers

Books by Cindi Myers

DO ME RIGHT
Cindi Myers

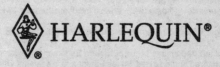

HARLEQUIN®

TORONTO • NEW YORK • LONDON
AMSTERDAM • PARIS • SYDNEY • HAMBURG
STOCKHOLM • ATHENS • TOKYO • MILAN • MADRID
PRAGUE • WARSAW • BUDAPEST • AUCKLAND

For Mike and Diane

ISBN 0-373-79184-4

DO ME RIGHT

Copyright © 2005 by Cynthia Myers.

www.eHarlequin.com

Printed in U.S.A.

1

AH, NOTHING LIKE A LITTLE confrontation to start off a gorgeous April morning. A block away from her shop, Austin Body Art, Theresa Jacobs stopped and frowned at the half-dozen picketers milling around the tattoo parlor.

Keep Austin Clean one of their signs read. Take Back Sixth Street proclaimed another. Stamp Out Smut said a third. She had to hand it to them—these folks didn't give up easily. They'd been out here every day for the last two weeks.

Two of the group wore oversize white T-shirts with the words Vote Darryl "Clean" Carter For Austin City Council. Ah, yes, "Clean" Carter. Self-appointed protector of citizen morals and champion of a family-friendly Austin. Apparently he'd decided that running Theresa and others like her out of business would be the ideal way to win his campaign.

Apparently Mr. Carter didn't realize how stubborn smut-sellers like her could be. She shifted her bag up higher on her shoulder and tugged her leather halter top down a little lower. Cleavage exposed—check. Belly-button ring showing—check. High-heeled boots, black fishnet hose, leather miniskirt—check. Big hair—check. Red, red lips—check. If Carter's minions expected sex, sin and sensation, she didn't want to disappoint them.

Sultry smile in place, she started toward the shop once more, moving in an exaggerated strut that had her hips swaying like a clock pendulum.

As they had each morning for the past two weeks, the protesters stopped and stared at her approach. "Good morning," she said, flashing a big smile as she inserted her key in the front-door lock.

"Good morn—" One of the men, a round, balding fellow with wire-rimmed glasses, started to return her greeting, but was cut off by an elbow in the ribs from the stern-faced woman in matching wire rims at his side.

"We're having a special today, folks," Theresa said. "Half-priced piercings. I know you won't want to miss that."

"You ought to be ashamed of yourself." A tall woman with hair the color of apricots stepped forward. "What if you had a daughter who dressed and acted the way you do?"

Theresa lowered her sunglasses and looked the woman up and down. "I'd say she was having a lot more fun than someone who dressed and acted the way *you* do."

On this exit line, she entered the shop and punched in her alarm code. Another day of fun and excitement at Austin Body Art. If only the moral dictators out there realized how mundane most of her life—and her clients—really were. She might look like a wild woman, but lately an exciting evening for her was a cable movie and Lean Cuisine.

She let the cats, Mick and Delilah, out of the back room. They protested their confinement loudly and wove in and out of her ankles until she filled their bowls with kibble. Then she switched on lights, booted up the computer and prepared to start the day.

Ten minutes later the door burst open. "Love you, too,

baby!" Her co-worker, Scott, blew kisses to the group outside, the effect somewhat spoiled by the one-finger salute he gave with his other hand. He slammed the door and turned to Theresa. "Don't those people ever give up?"

She shook her head. "They'll be gone after the election, one way or another."

Scott looked unconvinced. "You don't know what money and an agenda can do for a candidate." He glanced toward the group outside the front window. "These people are really fired up."

"If Carter wins, the picketers will still go away. And he may not like us, but he can't do anything about us. We're a legitimate, legal business."

"Yeah, but you can't stay in business long if you don't have customers, can you?" He slumped onto the stool behind the front counter and raked one hand through his spiked blond hair.

She ignored the twinge of fear his words produced. "What do you mean? Of course we'll have customers. Why wouldn't we?"

He shook his head. "I don't know. This Clean Up Austin drive is really cutting down on traffic. Business is taking a hit all over."

"We're still doing okay." They'd been a little slower, maybe, but every business had downtimes. "Things will pick up again soon. We don't have to worry."

"The Hot Tamale's already cutting staff." He rested his elbows on the counter, head in his hands. "I got laid off from my bartending gig last night."

"Oh, Scott." She set aside the mail she'd been sorting and went to him. "That sucks."

He nodded. "Yeah. And I just moved into that new apartment, too."

"You can work full-time here now, if you like."

He raised his head. "You mean it?"

"Sure. With Zach in Chicago, I could use the extra help." She glanced at the framed oil painting hanging over the cash register, a rendition of the Navy Pier in pop-art colors that was Zach's latest work. Big bro was having a blast in the Windy City while she was trying to keep it together here at home.

"But didn't you already hire someone else?"

"Another part-timer. She starts next week. But I could still use you full-time."

He glanced toward the front window again. The picketers had resumed their march up and down the sidewalk. "I don't know…."

"It'll be all right. At least give it a try."

"Okay. Thanks."

The news that the Hot Tamale, one of the street's most popular bars, was cutting staff stunned her. She'd known Carter's campaign was getting a lot of attention in the press, but she'd assumed most people wouldn't take him seriously. After all, Austin was known for its music scene and the nightlife on Sixth Street. Why would anyone want to take away the very thing that made the city so unique?

Obviously she'd underestimated the ability of a few soreheads to spoil the fun for everyone.

"Guess Zach picked a good time to skip town, huh?" Scott said. "Think he'll ever come back?"

She shrugged. "He still has another year and a half of school." And who knew where he'd end up after that. Before her brother followed Jen Truitt to Chicago a little over six months ago, he'd handed her the keys to Austin Body Art and told her the business was all hers. He wouldn't have done that if he'd planned to return anytime soon.

"I can see that cheered you right up." Scott slid off the stool. "I'll go make coffee."

As Scott disappeared into the back room, the bells on the front door jangled. Theresa turned to greet the two men who entered.

It would probably be more appropriate to say the men *made an entrance*. The first one was a tall drink of water in scuffed boots, sharply creased Wranglers, a denim shirt and a straw hat tilted low on his forehead. He strode into the room like a marshal stepping into a saloon in an old western. Broad-shouldered, narrow-waisted with a strong chin and a slightly crooked nose, he was movie-star handsome. She blinked a few times to make sure he was even real, wishing he'd take off the hat so she could get a look at his eyes. Not that she was interested in the average cowboy, but she could appreciate a gorgeous man as much as the next girl. "What can I do for you, gentlemen?" she asked.

His companion, a short, bow-legged man in a Bull Riders Stay On Longer T-shirt, removed his hat and stared openmouthed at the neckline of her halter top.

The taller man slapped his companion on the back of the head. "Put your eyes back in your skull and answer the lady."

His words broke the spell his initial appearance had cast over her, and for the first time she noticed the cast on his left forearm. The bright blue gauze wrapping made a sharp contrast to his deeply tanned skin.

He nodded to her and nudged his hat up enough for her to see his whiskey-colored eyes glinting with good humor.

To her astonishment and utter mortification, she felt her heart flutter. She had to force back the smile she knew would have looked ridiculously goofy. Adonis here was no doubt used to women swooning at his feet, and she didn't intend to be one of them.

"I apologize for my friend. He's not used to associating with females other than cows and horses," Handsome Hank continued.

"Shut your gob, Kyle." The shorter cowboy rubbed the back of his neck and focused his gaze somewhere over Theresa's left shoulder. "I'm interested in a tattoo."

"Then you came to the right place." With businesslike briskness, she plucked a clipboard from the rack by the counter and handed it to him. "Fill this out and we'll get started."

"Oh. Okay."

While he sat and began filling out the information and release form, she turned to his friend, Kyle. He was watching her, a speculative look in his eyes. The intensity of his gaze unnerved her. "Do you want a tattoo, too?"

The slow smile that formed on his lips would have knocked a lesser woman off her feet. As it was, Theresa took a step back and put one hand on the counter to steady herself.

"That's okay. Us naturally good-looking folks don't need any extra decoration." His gaze swept over the tiger etched on her shoulder, then shifted to the Celtic knot between her breasts. His smile broadened. "Though I have to say, you give me a whole new appreciation for your, um, art."

She laughed. "I'm sure you're a real art lover." She nodded to his cast. "What happened?"

He frowned at the injury. "Had a little trouble with an uncooperative bovine."

"Kyle has lousy luck with cattle and women." The shorter man, whose name turned out to be George, stood and handed Theresa the clipboard.

"Don't mind him," Kyle said. "He's been tossed on his head by bulls one too many times."

"You're a bull rider?" Theresa scanned the release form. Everything looked okay.

"Yes, ma'am." George threw back his shoulders and puffed out his chest. "I'm in the top fifteen on the circuit right now."

She glanced at Kyle. "Are you a bull rider, too?"

He shook his head. "No, I have more sense."

"He's too tall to ride bulls," George said. "He's a calf roper." He glanced at the arm. "Or was."

"I can still whip you with one arm tied behind my back."

She somehow refrained from rolling her eyes at this typical male posturing. Honestly, was she supposed to be impressed? Better keep her mind on business. "Do you know what you want for your tat?" she asked George.

"I want a big lizard." He pointed to his forearm. "Right here."

"A lizard?"

He nodded. "'Cause that's my handle on the circuit. George 'the Lizard' Lizardi."

"Okay." She led him to a thick binder on a stand by the counter and flipped through it until she came to the reptile section. "You ought to find something here."

Scott emerged from the back room with two mugs of coffee. "Y'all want coffee?" he asked.

"That'd be nice," Kyle said.

"None for me," George said. "I'm jumpy enough."

"George is a little nervous about needles," Kyle said.

Theresa nodded. "He'll be fine once we get started. For most people the anticipation of getting a tattoo is a lot more uncomfortable than the tat itself."

"What's your name?"

The question was a reasonable one, but it still caught her off guard. She started to ask him why he was interested, then thought better of it. He was a customer, or at least a buddy of a customer, so she ought to be polite. "Theresa Jacobs," she said. "And you're Kyle."

"Kyle Cameron." He offered his good hand. "Pleased to meet you, Theresa."

His hand was warm, his grasp firm but not painful, calluses scraping against her palm. A masculine hand, telegraphing strength and confidence. Her heart fluttered again, and she jerked away and fussed with the supplies on the cart, though her skin still tingled from his touch.

Scott returned with another mug of coffee, followed by Mick and Delilah. True to her name, Delilah zeroed in on the handsome cowboy and began rubbing against his boots, purring loudly.

Kyle regarded the cat with a half smile. "Cute cat."

"She's all right." She nudged Delilah away with the toe of her boot, then moved to a supply cart and began laying out the materials she'd need for the tattoo—sealed packets of needles, fresh ink caps, gauze, sterile wipes, A & D ointment and the tattoo machine, still in its sealed packet from the autoclave.

"I've never been around cats much." He followed her and leaned back against the workbench. "My sister has them."

"These were my brother's until he moved to Chicago."

"What's he doing in Chicago?"

"Going to school." And falling even more madly in love with Jen Truitt. The thought still amazed her—her tough-stuff big brother all mushy in love with the police chief's daughter. Who would have thought?

"I found the one I want." George pointed to a page in the binder.

Theresa walked over and studied the drawing of a snarling monitor lizard. One of Zach's designs. "All right. Have a seat in the chair and we'll get started."

Looking a little apprehensive, George stretched out in the chair. "You want me to hold your hand?" Kyle asked.

"Only if you want me to break the other arm."

While she prepped George, Kyle settled on a stool across from them. "So what's with the chapel meeting outside?" he asked.

She swabbed the freshly shaved section of George's arm with disinfectant and positioned the tattoo transfer. "The Clean Up Austin campaign? Haven't you heard of them?"

He shook his head. "Until I hurt my arm I was riding the circuit, trying to earn enough points to make the national finals."

She began filling ink caps from larger bottles on the stand beside her. "This guy, Darryl 'Clean' Carter, is running for Austin City Council. His campaign platform is that he intends to make Austin—and particularly Sixth Street—

more family friendly, which means no tattoo parlors, strip joints, sex-toy stores or loud rock-and-roll bars. Only nice, staid restaurants, suitably quiet taverns and fun for the whole family." She rolled her eyes and unwrapped a fresh tattoo needle. "I think it's ridiculous, but they've been out there every morning for the past two weeks." She switched on the tattoo machine. "You ready, George?"

"Uh, yeah." He blanched. "Sure."

"Don't worry, pard. When you pass out from the pain, I'll help revive you." Kyle winked at Theresa, who steadfastly ignored the way this made her stomach quiver and concentrated on the tattoo.

George made a gurgling sound in his throat when the needle first made contact. She kept a firm grip on his arm and continued working. "Take a deep breath. Relax. Focus on something else to distract you."

Predictably his gaze zeroed in on her chest once more. "Th-that's a real interesting tattoo," he said. "Who did it?"

"My brother."

"He's a tattoo artist, too?" Kyle asked.

"He's the one who taught me."

"I was wondering how a pretty girl like you would get into something like this," George said.

"Right." She switched colors and began outlining the lizard's eyes. "Like I haven't heard that one before."

"I don't know. Sounds like a pretty good job to me," Kyle said. "Good hours. You're pretty much your own boss." He grinned. "And a chance to inflict pain on ugly SOBs like the Lizard here."

"Don't give her any ideas," George protested.

As she worked, she could feel Kyle's eyes on her. His

stare wasn't the rude ogling of some men but rather the studious gaze of someone who was trying to figure her out. Ogling, she could deal with—she didn't much care for this kind of close scrutiny. "Do you mind?" she said, glaring at him.

"Mind what?"

"You're staring."

"No, I'm watching you."

"Well, stop it."

"You interest me."

"Well, cowboys don't interest me, so don't get any ideas."

"Darlin', I've had ideas about you since the minute I laid eyes on you."

The combination of a molasses-sweet drawl and a one-hundred-degree gaze was doing a number on her libido. She maintained her grip on the tattoo machine and continued working, the original Ms. Cool. "You and your ideas are going to be very disappointed," she said, ignoring the pinch of regret the words sent through her.

He laughed. "You've done it now."

"Done what?" Why did he look so pleased with himself?

"Saying that's like waving a red flag in front of a bull. There's nothing a man like me enjoys better than a challenge."

She bristled. "That wasn't a challenge."

"Sounded like one to me," George said.

She looked from one man to the other. They were both wearing smart-ass grins. She had half a mind to slap sense into both of them. But that would probably only egg them on. She settled for a return to her ice-queen routine. "Think what you like," she said. "You'll end up disappointed."

As someone who'd had her share of disappointments, she knew they'd learn to live with it.

KYLE WATCHED THERESA WORK. He couldn't remember when he'd met a more intriguing package: sex appeal and sass wrapped up with a heavy dose of smarts.

He was glad he'd let George talk him into coming here this morning instead of sitting around in his borrowed apartment, moping the way he'd done ever since that sidewinder of a calf had snapped the bone in his wrist and put an abrupt halt to this season's rodeo competition.

All he had to look forward to now was six weeks of bumming around town or, worse, recuperating at the family ranch, listening to his sister's lectures on responsibility and settling down, enduring her transparent attempts at matchmaking and sidestepping her pointed questions about his plans for the future.

"What do you do when you're not on the rodeo circuit?" Theresa's question pulled him away from his fast slide toward a deep blue funk. She was focusing on the lizard taking shape on George's arm, not looking at him, but apparently she'd decided to at least be friendly.

"My family has a ranch out near Wimberley," he said. "I'm supposed to be living there and helping out, but right now I'm just hanging out around Austin. I've got a friend who's working on an oil rig in Nigeria and he's letting me stay at his apartment until he comes home." He'd sent his horse to the ranch right after the accident, but he wasn't exactly eager to set up headquarters there himself.

"Oh. So you really are a cowboy."

"I guess you could say that."

"Kyle's folks have been raising cattle and horses for at least four generations," George said. "Ain't that right?"

"Yeah. The Two Ks has been around just about forever."

"I guess that's a really cool thing," Theresa said. "But I think I'd be bored out of my skull living way out like that." She shut off the tattoo machine and blotted George's fresh tat with gauze. "Guess I'm too much of a city girl."

You and me both, Kyle thought, but he kept quiet. His current restlessness didn't really have anything to do with this woman, though he couldn't help wondering if she or someone like her wouldn't be a good antidote to what was ailing him. Spending the next six weeks having a good time with a willing woman would be a damn sight more fun than moping around the ranch house dodging his sister's nagging to persuade him to settle down.

"What time do you get off work?" he asked.

She looked up, the hard look erased from her face for a moment. For a split second she looked softer. Vulnerable even. Then the mask was back in place. "I told you I wasn't interested."

He let a slow smile form, putting every bit of sex appeal he could muster into the look. Women had told him before that he was charming. He only hoped Theresa agreed. "I think I could make things interesting…for both of us."

"Aw, come on. Are you two going to sit there making goo-goo eyes at each other, or are you gonna finish my tattoo?"

George's whine effectively broke whatever had been building between them. Lips pressed together in a thin line, Theresa bandaged George's arm and gave him a list of instructions for caring for his tattoo.

While George paid his bill, Kyle looked around. A sign by the cash register announced the hours of business as eleven to eleven weekdays. That meant he had about ten hours to kill before he could make his next move.

2

THERESA CHECKED HER WATCH as she turned the key in the dead bolt of the shop. Almost midnight. Time for Cinderella to turn back into a scullery maid. Time for her to head home.

To what? Not even a cat waited for her at her apartment. No one would call to make sure she'd arrived safely. No one would ask about her day or be ready to keep her company in bed.

She'd never minded her solitary life before. She had friends, and though she hadn't had a serious relationship with a man in years, she hadn't really wanted one. She never lacked for companionship whenever she was interested. But since Zach had moved away, there was no one she was really close to.

Suddenly the last place she wanted to be was that empty apartment. She turned in the opposite direction from the lot where she'd parked her car and headed back up East Sixth.

At this hour the protestors were gone, but the crowds were thin even for a weeknight. How much of this was due to Clean Carter's campaign? What would happen to the businesses on the street if this kept up?

She was probably worrying over nothing. She'd grab a bite to eat, wind down a little, then head home. A good night's sleep would pull her out of the bad mood she'd been in all day.

She pushed open the door to the Library Bar and went inside. "Hey, Pete." She greeted the bartender and took a seat at the bar. "Any pizza left?"

"Couple of slices." Pete took a glass from over his head and filled it with ice. "Diet Coke?"

"Yeah. And a slice of pizza." She looked around the room. Two couples occupied tables across the room and three college-age guys sat at the other end of the bar watching a television with the sound turned down.

"Quiet in here tonight," she said as he set the drink in front of her.

"It's been quiet in here a lot of nights lately. People don't want to deal with being hassled by a bunch of sign-waving, pamphlet-pushing busybodies. What about at your place?"

She shrugged. She'd had less than a dozen customers all day, all regulars except for George and Kyle.

She shifted, trying to get more comfortable on the hard bar stool. She'd been thinking about Kyle off and on all day. She couldn't remember the last time a man had gotten her attention the way the handsome cowboy had.

Some of her friends had accused her of being too picky; she preferred to think of it as particular. If she was going to spend her time and energy on a man, she wanted to be sure he was worth the trouble.

Kyle had definitely sparked her interest. He had a cocky self-assurance that challenged her to tame him and enough of a sense of humor to hint at fun along the way. In her experience, the combination could be incendiary in bed—and impossible out of it.

Pete delivered her pizza and she began to eat. As she chewed, she couldn't help thinking that a dinner that was the equivalent of rubbery cheese on cardboard was a sure sign of a miserable social life.

"You don't look like you're enjoying that much."

Startled, she dropped the half-eaten pizza slice and stared at the man who'd slid onto the bar stool next to her. "What are you doing here?"

Kyle tilted his hat back on his head. "I'm looking for you."

Whatever appetite she'd had deserted her at those four words. She pushed her plate away and took a long drink, careful not to look at him, though she could feel his gaze burning into her. "Why would you be looking for me?"

She waited for some flirty or suggestive answer, but he remained silent. She held out for a full minute, but after that she had to look at him. He wasn't smiling—in fact, he looked far too serious.

Pete approached. "What can I get you?"

"Bourbon and Coke." Kyle turned to Theresa. "Do you want anything else?"

She shook her head. What she wanted was to get out of here. Away from him and the shaky, unsettled way he made her feel.

"How long have you been a tattoo artist?" he asked.

The very ordinariness of the question surprised her. No innuendo or playfulness, just ordinary conversation. What was he up to? She shifted slightly away from him and stirred her drink with the straw. "About seven years now. I apprenticed a couple years before that."

"Uh-huh. I've been on the rodeo circuit ten years. A long time to be smelling horse shit and wrestling ornery cows."

"If you don't enjoy it anymore, why don't you quit?"

He nodded. "I've been thinking about that. But I don't see a lot of other options. It's what I'm used to."

"You can't rodeo with your arm in a cast, can you?"

"There is that." He frowned at his injured forearm, then took a long drink. "I've been doing a lot of thinking about what I'm going to do with myself for the next six weeks, until I can get back on the circuit."

So he was grounded for six weeks? A lot could happen in that kind of time.

She pushed the thought away. She didn't want anything to do with a randy cowboy. She looked away, pretending indifference. "I don't see how I can help you there."

He scooted closer. "Oh, but I think you can." His voice was a notch above a whisper; velvet brushed across nerves set on hyperalert. "I think you and I could make the next six weeks damned interesting."

Try as she might, she couldn't keep back the hot flush that swept up her neck and across her cheeks. "Forget it," she said, even as she listened for him to elaborate.

He traced his forefinger down her arm. "Hear me out, now. I believe we'd both benefit from what I have in mind."

"What could you possibly do for me, cowboy?" Watching the light and shadows play across his handsome face, half a dozen erotic ideas flitted through her mind. But they were just ideas—she was better off not getting involved.

"For one thing, I could take you out and buy you a better dinner than stale bar pizza." He thumped the plate containing the remains of her meal.

"I don't need you to take me to dinner," she said.

"But what about after dinner?" He stroked her cheek, a

silken touch that immediately raised her temperature five degrees. "Maybe you need me then."

"No, I don't," she said, even though her body had other ideas.

"I think you do." He leaned closer still, so that his knee met hers and his arm brushed the side of her breast. "And I sure as hell need you. The minute I laid eyes on you this afternoon, I knew we'd be good together."

"You're dreaming." When did it get to be so warm in here? Maybe she should ask Pete to turn down the air-conditioning. Or she could go home—now—and take a cold shower.

"If I'm dreaming, then it's a wet dream, darlin'." He smoothed her hair behind her ear. "Don't tell me you don't feel it, too."

"Feel what?" Somehow she managed to get the words out around the knot in her throat.

"These sparks between us. Our bodies are saying things to each other. Don't you want to finish the conversation?"

"You've been drinking too much."

He pushed his half-empty glass away. "Not nearly enough to get you out of my mind."

"I'm not interested in getting involved with you or anyone else," she said.

"It depends on what you mean by *involved*." He sat up straighter. "I'm talking about six weeks of enjoying each other. No strings attached. We both make the best of it."

"I'm not interested." She laid a five on the counter and stood to leave.

He touched her arm lightly. "Don't be so hasty. I've done a little checking. Discreetly. I know you're not involved with anyone else."

"I like it that way."

"Really?" His gaze pierced her, challenging her to admit the truth. "You don't look like a woman who's made to be celibate."

"Oh, so you're going to save me from that fate? How noble of you!"

"Nothing noble about it. Like I said before, we'd both benefit from a few weeks of fun."

She shook her head. "Find somebody else."

"I don't want somebody else. I want you."

The man didn't mince words, she had to give him that. Would he be as direct in bed? "Why me?"

He stood, pressing in close, scant inches between them. "You intrigue me. You've got brains to go with that sexy body." He smoothed his hand down her arm. "We wouldn't bore each other."

Men had called her a lot of things, but *smart* wasn't usually one of them. The idea that he saw past her vamp wardrobe and tough-girl attitude moved her more than she cared to admit.

And the fact that he could snare her this easily frightened her. She pulled away. "I have to go now."

"All right. I'll walk you to your car."

"You don't have to do that."

"I insist." He fell into step beside her. He said nothing as they exited the bar and walked down the deserted street, but every part of her was aware of him. As tall as she was, he was taller. He walked next to the street, touching her elbow to guide her around obstacles, pausing at the corner to look both ways before escorting her across the street. She couldn't remember when she'd felt so protected. She told herself she ought to bristle at such condescending behavior, but the truth was, it felt good to be looked after this way, as if he thought she deserved a little extra care.

She took out her keys as they reached her car, suddenly feeling awkward. What do you say to a man whose proposition you've just turned down? *Thanks* didn't seem quite appropriate. "Well, good night and goodbye."

"Good night. But I won't say goodbye." He reached out and pulled her close. "I'll definitely be seeing you again." She only had time to gasp before his lips met hers.

Her first thought was that this was a man who knew his way around a kiss. His mouth was firm against hers but not forceful, his hands sliding down her arms gently even as his tongue coaxed her to respond. He tasted of smoky whiskey and sweet cola, and smelled like starched cotton, oiled leather and male musk. The taste and scent and feel of him—his hot, exploring mouth and firm, unyielding muscle and gentle hands—battered at her last shreds of resistance. She melted against him, her surrendering moan muffled by his seeking mouth.

The heat that had smoldered between them all evening crackled into flames. She pressed against him, standing on tiptoe, both hands cradling the back of his head, her fingers sliding through his thick hair, pulling him closer still. She reveled in the scrape of his beard against her chin, the pressure of his belt buckle against her stomach. Suddenly every passing second reminded her how long she'd been alone and how much she didn't want to be by herself anymore.

And then the spell was over. He raised his head and moved out of her arms. They stood inches apart, staring at each other, gasping for breath. His stunned expression mirrored her feelings.

She blinked, fighting to keep her composure. What had just happened? Had she really lost control like that with a man she hardly knew?

She hugged her arms over her chest and rubbed her shoulders, fighting a sudden chill and the longing to have his arms around her again. "I have to go," she said.

This time he didn't try to stop her. But as she started the car and reached to pull the door shut, he leaned in. "I'll see you soon, darlin'," he said in that warm, molasses voice that was guaranteed to keep her hot and bothered for the rest of the night.

KYLE MANAGED TO HOLD IT together until Theresa's car was out of sight. Then he slumped against an adjacent car and removed his hat to wipe the sweat from his brow.

What exactly had happened just now? He'd meant to kiss her, but he hadn't expected spontaneous combustion. He'd come dangerously close to laying her back across the hood of her car and taking her right there.

He smiled, remembering her feeble denials that there wasn't anything between them. One kiss had shown her for a liar. Next time she'd have to find another excuse to refuse him.

Judging by the way she'd melted in his arms just now, she wouldn't say no much longer. He stared down the empty street in the direction she'd driven, wondering what his next move would be. On the one hand, he could show up at her shop tomorrow and continue to play the game—flirting and touching, daring her to give in to her feelings and give herself up to six weeks of very physical therapy that would benefit them both.

On the other hand, a little voice in his head was telling him to turn around and run the other way. A woman like Theresa Jacobs didn't ever really surrender. Women like her took prisoners. With one kiss, he was already halfway snared in her web. Not exactly a good beginning for a casual alliance. He wanted fun without forfeit, a way to give his body without worrying about his heart. One look at Theresa, with her tattoos and leather, her overt sex appeal and go-to-hell attitude, and he thought he'd found the perfect partner to help occupy his time while he was forced to remain close to home.

Now he wasn't so sure about what he'd thought was a brilliant plan.

He straightened and headed back toward the bar. Maybe a stiff drink, or a few stiff drinks, would drown out his doubts. But he doubted he'd see clearly through an alcoholic haze, or know any better what he should do if he woke in the morning with a hangover. So he detoured past the Library Bar and headed for the lot where he'd parked his truck. Gold's Gym was open twenty-four hours. A few miles on the treadmill or lifting weights with his good hand might clear his head.

Or at least wear him out enough to sleep without dreaming of a certain leather-clad siren and a single scorching kiss.

EVERY LAMP IN HER APARTMENT couldn't cast enough light to drive out the dark mood that had enveloped Theresa by the time she arrived home. Damn Kyle Cameron for making her feel this way! She'd been fine until he'd come along and decided to take her along on his little ego trip. She might have been a little lonely, but she'd been okay. At least she hadn't been bothered by the restlessness that grated at her now.

She dropped her purse on the counter, then strode into the bedroom, shedding boots and stockings along the way. By the time she reached the bathroom, she was down to a purple silk thong.

She poured a generous amount of lavender-and-vanilla bubble bath into the old-fashioned claw-foot tub and turned both taps on full. A soak in the tub was bound to relax her enough so she could sleep. In the morning, she'd be able to make more sense of her feelings.

She turned and caught sight of herself in the mirror and froze, studying her reflection with a critical eye. Two years shy of thirty, she was holding up well. Though she enjoyed eating too much to be overly skinny, she had an hourglass shape men appreciated, with definite curves she wasn't afraid to show off. Her tattoos were artistic, not overwhelming: a snarling tiger on her left shoulder, a band of flowers around her right bicep, the Chinese symbol for courage on her right ankle.

Her full breasts were still firm, the Celtic knot a lacy etching between them. Her nipples were dark against her pale skin and erect now in the coolness of the apartment. She smoothed her hand down her sides, watching the nipples pucker further at her touch.

She lowered her gaze to her stomach, slightly rounded and soft but not fat or flabby. A gold *T* dangled from the ring in her navel, a single diamond chip winking in its center.

She slid her thumbs beneath the narrow waistband of the thong and skimmed it down her thighs, watching herself in the mirror. Her dark pubic hair was trimmed close, an inch-wide strip down the center. She wondered what Kyle would think if he could see that. Would the sight of her naked excite him?

She'd felt him tonight, the ridge of his erection hard between them. He'd been hard all over, really, muscles like iron holding her with surprising tenderness. She grew damp at the memory.

Once the tub had filled, she turned off the taps and slid beneath the bubbles. The warm water caressed her and she sighed, breathing in the rich perfume of lavender and vanilla. Eyes closed, she willed herself to relax. This was her sanctuary, a place where worries were banished.

But even this treasured ritual couldn't erase thoughts of the kiss she'd shared with Kyle. The moment was seared into her brain. As soon as she closed her eyes, she saw him again, his lips curved in a lethal half smile, his eyes assessing her, stripping her bare.

But it was his touch that had been her undoing. The memory of his lips and hands on her still burned her, awakening feelings that had lain dormant too long.

She slid soap-slicked hands up to cover her breasts, rubbing back and forth across aching nipples. It was a poor substitute for what she really wanted—a man's hands, *Kyle's* hands, on her.

Imagining it was Kyle's hands she was guiding, she moved lower, across her stomach, down between her legs. She pretended it was his fingers parting her folds to stroke her clit, his body satisfying the desire building within her.

Our bodies are saying things to each other. Don't you want to finish the conversation? His words returned to her, fuel to the fire burning inside her. If a man could get her this hot with only the memory of his voice, what would happen if she invited him into her bed?

She arched up, anticipating release, water sloshing over the sides of the tub. Her cries echoed in the room as her climax overtook her. Eyes closed, she sank down in the tub again. She'd found physical release but nothing like what she really wanted. What she really needed.

3

KYLE WAITED A DAY BEFORE going back to Austin Body Art, telling himself he wanted to give Theresa time to think about his proposition. Time to remember the lip-scorching kiss they'd shared and contemplate what that kind of kiss might lead to once they got their clothes off.

In reality, he felt the need of a little cooling-off period himself. He was sure he could handle anything Theresa threw at him, but he had to admit he'd never been involved with someone who made a living poking people with needles. Not to mention one who'd practically melted his bones with a single kiss. He needed to rest up for his next move.

The picketers were patrolling the sidewalk in front of the tattoo parlor when he returned to the shop. "Sir, you should read this!" An earnest-looking woman shoved a flyer into his hand as he reached for the door of the shop.

Printed on blaze-orange paper, the flyer read "Keep Austin clean! Take back the streets for our children! Fight for a family-friendly Austin! Vote for Darryl 'Clean' Carter for City Council Place Four!!"

"Nice exclamation marks," he said, attempting to hand the paper back to the woman.

"Oh, no. You keep it." She frowned at his hand on the doorknob. "You don't really want to go in there, do you?"

"I don't?" He removed his hand from the doorknob and turned to face her. "Why not?" He looked at the others, who had stopped marching with their signs and gathered around like buzzards waiting for their turn at the dead armadillo on the side of the road. "What is y'all's objection to this place?"

"This isn't the kind of thing children should be exposed to." A man in a dark suit and helmet hair stepped forward. "It's morally repugnant and encourages overt sexuality and flaunting of the body."

"Brushed up on those vocabulary words, did you?" Kyle grinned and made a show of looking around them. "I don't see any children here, do you?" He scratched his head. "Guess they're all at home, watching sex and violence on TV."

The man glared at him. "This is not something to be made light of," he said.

"Right." Kyle turned and grasped the doorknob again. "Don't wear yourselves out toting those signs or anything."

The string of bells on the back of the door announced his entrance into the shop. One of the cats, curled up in a chair by the door, blinked at him sleepily. The blond dude who'd been there the other day looked up from the computer behind the front counter. "Can I help you?"

"I just stopped by to see Theresa."

At the sound of her name, she looked up from her seat next to the tattoo chair. She shut off the machine and blotted the partial tattoo on the back of the man who reclined beside her. "Kyle, what are you doing here?"

Was it his imagination or was her voice a little breathy? He strode into the room and lowered himself into a folding chair near her work area. "I came to see you, of course."

He nodded to the man, a middle-aged biker type with a long, gray pigtail and grease-stained jeans. "Don't let me interrupt."

She switched on the machine again. "Eric, this is Kyle. If you don't want him to watch, I'll tell him to leave."

Eric raised his head and looked Kyle up and down. "Don't make no difference to me," he said and lowered his head again.

Theresa turned her attention back to the tattoo, which was fine with Kyle, as it gave him the chance to watch her. A pair of fine lines creased her forehead as she concentrated on her work. The design taking shape beneath her hand was intricate and colorful: a whole garden full of roses surrounding some sort of fantastic bird—a phoenix, maybe—in brilliant reds, greens, blues and yellows. She was working on the bird now, inking in the tail feathers.

Bent over like this, he had a terrific view of the tops of her breasts swelling at the neck of the leather vest she wore. Some kind of flower or design was tattooed in her cleavage. He was definitely interested in getting a closer look at that....

"Shouldn't you be back at the ranch punching cows or something?"

Her voice pulled him out of the beginning of a very interesting fantasy. He raised his eyes to meet hers. "We don't punch 'em anymore," he drawled. "We just suggest they move 'long. It's more PC that way."

Eric made a choking sound, but Kyle soon realized it was a chuckle, muffled by his position. "I'm going to remember that one," the biker said. "What happened to your arm?"

After less than a week, the question was already getting

old. He looked at the blue-wrapped cast. "One of the cows punched back."

The biker laughed again. "You're a riot."

"Guess if the rodeo gig doesn't work out, I can be a stand-up comic in a biker bar," he said.

Theresa apparently didn't appreciate his humor. She was still frowning. "What *have* you been doing since you got hurt? Just sitting around on your ass?"

He winced. That was a low blow. Just because he was twenty-nine years old and didn't have a real job didn't mean he was a bum. "I'm exploring my options," he said.

"Hmmph." But the slight flush to her cheeks made him think she was remembering how he'd asked her to help him pass the time while he was recuperating.

He sat back, hands behind his head. "I thought about taking up panhandling," he said. "But there seems to be a glut of people in that line of work around here lately. Then I heard they were auditioning for Chippendales dancers, so I thought about strapping on my chaps and giving it a go." He gave an exaggerated shimmy. "What do you say, darlin'? Think I've got what it takes?"

Aha! She looked! He deliberately licked his lips. He'd be happy to show her he had what it would take to please her.

"Maybe we could hire him to run off those picketers," the blonde behind the counter said.

"I don't think one beat-up cowboy's going to scare them much," she said.

If he thought she really meant the words, he might have been insulted. But the very way she avoided looking at him told him she was all too aware of his presence. He liked that. She didn't look like the kind of woman who was easily unnerved, but he'd managed to get to her. Score one for the cowboy, beat-up or not.

"Besides, it's a free country," Theresa continued. "We can't stop them from walking on the sidewalk."

"Screw 'em," Eric said. "They don't know what they're missing."

"They don't have much of a sense of humor, do they?" Kyle leaned forward, elbows on his knees. "A guy out there told me this place 'encourages overt sexuality and flaunting of the body.' Like that was a bad thing."

"Hey, if you've got it, flaunt it," the blonde said, flexing a scrawny arm.

"Sounds good to me." Kyle's gaze lingered on Theresa's inviting cleavage once more. "What do you think, Theresa?"

She switched off the machine and patted Eric's shoulder. "I think that's all for today," she said. "Next time I'll do the talons and finish up the pyramid at the bottom."

"Thanks, T," the biker said. He raised up on his elbows while she cleaned and dressed the fresh tattoo. "You here for a tattoo?" he asked.

Kyle shook his head. "No, I'm just here to harass Theresa. I know how much she loves it." There went that blush again, the slightest pink along her cheekbones. It was immensely gratifying and sexy as hell.

Eric dressed and left. Kyle got up and walked over to where Theresa was cleaning off her work space. "I've been thinking about you," he said softly.

Her shoulders stiffened, but she kept on working. Pretending to ignore him.

He smoothed his hands down her upper arms. "I've been thinking about the way you kissed me."

She shrugged out of his grasp and moved over to the workbench. "I didn't kiss you. *You* kissed *me*."

He followed. "Ah, but you kissed me back."

She stripped off her latex gloves and turned to face him. "So what if I did?" Her breasts rose and fell, almost brushing the front of his shirt, though whether she was breathing hard from anger or arousal, he couldn't tell.

"A woman who can kiss like that shouldn't be content with just a kiss." He resisted the urge to touch her again, and settled for staring into her eyes. They were dark brown, almost black, a shade lighter than her hair. Heavily lined in black, the lashes lush with mascara, her eyes looked exotic. Erotic as the rest of her. He shifted his stance to accommodate his growing erection. If she had any doubts about his reaction to her, one look would tell her all she needed to know. "Don't tell me you haven't been thinking about the proposition I made."

She glanced past him, over his shoulder. Too late he remembered the blonde at the cash register. "Scott, go ahead and go to lunch," she said.

"Now?"

"Yes, now. You don't have any appointments until three, do you?"

"Figures you'd run me off just when it was getting interesting." But he scooted his chair back.

A few moments later, the bells on the door sounded and they were alone. He reached for Theresa, intending to kiss her, but she scooted sideways, out of his grasp. "What's in it for me if I do agree to your proposition?" she asked.

He folded his arms across his chest and struck a casual pose against the workbench. "Oh, I don't think you'll be disappointed. The fireworks we set off the other night were just a little preview."

"Don't flatter yourself, cowboy."

He shrugged, ignoring the uneasy feeling in his gut. "What do you want?"

She bit her lip. Her uncertainty surprised him. She took a deep breath. "Okay, here's how it is. *If* I agree to do this, it's just you and me for six weeks. No other women on the side."

Easy enough. He nodded. "Darlin', I don't intend for either one of us to have *time* to see anyone else."

She hugged her arms across her breasts. "And you won't try to change me—not the way I dress or act or anything."

He looked her up and down. "I wouldn't change a thing."

"And no lies."

He blinked. "What would I lie about?"

"In my experience, some men will lie about anything. Just don't try it with me. If I find out you've lied, you *will* live to regret it."

He was starting to get a picture here of one or more lying, cheating, manipulative men she'd been involved with in the past. The thought of some bastard hurting her that way made him more than a little angry. "No lies from me," he said. "Believe it or not, all that stuff about truth, honor and the cowboy way isn't just hogwash."

She nodded, though she hadn't relaxed one bit. "All right then."

Not quite the enthusiastic response he'd been hoping for. "Is that a yes?"

"Come back tonight after closing." She turned and began rearranging things on the workbench. He stared at her back, at the leather miniskirt that clung to her shapely backside, at the fall of straight black hair that reached almost to her waist, at her shoulders hunched against him. That was it? An order to come back later?

"That's not the way to seal a bargain." He closed the gap between them in two strides and put his good hand on her waist, his mouth next to her ear. "We need to give each other something to mark the occasion."

She looked back at him with a puzzled expression. "You want me to give you a gift?"

He smiled at her confusion. He liked this version of her, soft and a little vulnerable, almost as much as he did the sexy, woman-in-charge side of her. Gently he turned her until she was facing him, her back against the workbench. He moved in closer, letting her feel exactly how much she turned him on. "A kiss will do," he said. "One kiss to give us both something to think about until tonight."

Her lips were every bit as soft as he remembered—soft and sensuous. He coaxed them apart and her tongue met his, sparring and retreating in an erotic dance. He sucked gently at her mouth and she responded, nipping at his upper lip, sending a jolt of heat straight to his groin.

With a sound that was part growl, part purr, she reached up and put her arms around his neck, her fingers tangling in his hair. She pressed her breasts to his chest and ground her pelvis against him. He slid his good hand down to cup her bottom, bringing her closer still. They were as close as they could be without being naked, and the sensation drove him half-crazy. To hell with waiting until tonight. They had a pretty comfortable-looking reclining chair right here....

Then, in an instant, it was over. She slipped out of his

arms and stepped back, one hand to her swollen lips, her breasts rising and falling as she struggled to control her breathing. "I-I'll see you tonight," she stammered.

He started to protest, then thought better of it. She'd laid down the rules, and for now he'd do best to follow them. He didn't want to risk her turning skittish and backing out of the deal. Not when he was on fire with wanting her. He took a step back, toward the door. "Yeah. Tonight."

Before he could change his mind, he turned and left, pushing past the protestors, ignoring their attempts to press more flyers on him. He had to get away from Theresa now, but he'd be counting the minutes until he saw her again.

"SO WHAT'S UP WITH YOU AND that cowboy?"

If Theresa had hoped Scott would forget about Kyle over lunch, she had no such luck. He'd returned fifteen minutes after Kyle left the shop, bearing a burger, fries and a Coke—and a lot of questions.

"It's personal," she said, settling at the table in the back room to eat her lunch.

He turned a chair around and straddled it. "That was obvious. How personal?"

"None of your business. Shouldn't you be up front, in case anyone comes in?"

"We can hear the bells from here." He rested his chin on his folded arms and studied her. "If you ask me, it's about time you hooked up with somebody. I don't think you were cut out to be a nun."

"What's that supposed to mean?"

He shrugged. "Just that ever since Zach left, you haven't

been in a very good mood. Getting laid might be just the thing to cheer you up."

She glared at him. "Who asked you?"

He laughed. "Hey, it always works for me."

"*Some* of us don't get off on sleeping around like a stray dog, okay?"

He preened, running a hand through his spiky bleached-blond hair. "Can I help it if women find me irresistible?"

She took a long drink of Coke and shook her head. "Some women have no taste."

"So tell me about this new employee you hired. Guy or gal?"

Grateful for the change in subject, she relaxed a little. "Female. She's a music major at UT."

"A musician who knows tattoos?" He grinned. "Does she play in a band?"

"I have no idea. Apparently her mom and dad have a shop in Denver. She grew up in the business."

"I can't wait to meet her. When does she start?"

"This afternoon."

He started to get up, but she leaned forward and grabbed his arm, squeezing hard. "Scott?"

"What?" Worry lines stood out on his high forehead.

"No hitting on the help, okay?"

"Just a little flirting…."

"Not if she's not interested in flirting back. That's sexual harassment and it could get us both sued."

She released him and he leaned back, rubbing his arm. "I won't do anything stupid," he said huffily. He shoved back the chair and left the room.

She contemplated her half-eaten sandwich. Of course

Scott would do something stupid. He couldn't help it. When a man's hormones took over, his brain stopped working. Simple as that.

She was one to talk though. She'd just agreed to what was probably a stupid idea. A fun fling with a cowboy stud. It sounded good on the surface, but who knew where that kind of thing could lead? Hadn't Zach and Jen's relationship started the same way?

At least theirs had worked out okay. She didn't have that kind of luck with men. For one thing, she wasn't the soft, girlie-girl type they seemed to prefer. Even the biker dudes she'd spent time with had accused her of being too tough. The last guy she'd spent more than one night with had said she was too bossy. Which maybe was true, but he'd liked it enough in the beginning.

That was a man for you. Not consistent. When she'd been younger and more naïve, she hadn't known that and it had gotten her into trouble. She wouldn't make that mistake again.

The bell on the door sounded. She didn't have an appointment until two, but maybe the customer was early. In any case, she'd lost her appetite for lunch. She wrapped up the rest of the sandwich and stashed it in the refrigerator, then went up front.

She found Scott talking with a petite girl with short red hair. She wore a long, flowing sundress and sandals, and had no visible piercings other than two studs in each ear. A sun-and-moon tattoo adorned her left shoulder.

"What's your name?" Scott was asking when Theresa joined them.

"Cherry. Cherry Donovan."

Scott's eyes lit up. "Cherry. Nice name."

She scowled at him. "No cracks about the name, okay?"

He held up both hands. His innocent expression wouldn't have fooled his grandmother. "Hey, I didn't say anything."

Cherry glanced at Theresa and rolled her eyes. "You thought it. Men always do."

Scott looked to Theresa for help. She held out her hand. "Hi, Cherry, good to see you again."

"Hey, Theresa. I'm a little early, but my class this afternoon was canceled, so I thought I'd come on by and spend a little time getting to know the place."

Cherry had a pretty smile and a vulnerable, elfin quality. Theresa felt like an Amazon. But the girl couldn't very well help that she was short, could she? "We're glad to have you here," she said. "I see you've already met Scott."

"So you're the new part-timer?" He grinned and stuck out his hand. "I'm Scott."

"That's what she just said." Cherry touched his hand briefly, then deftly moved away. Scott's face fell.

Theresa turned her head, biting her lip to keep from laughing. So much for Mr. Suave's chances with his new co-worker. Cherry was obviously less than impressed. "You pretty much saw everything when you interviewed, but I'll refresh your memory," Theresa said. She scooped up the cat that had been weaving around her boots. "This is Delilah. The other one, Mick, is around here somewhere."

"I remember." Cherry scratched underneath the cat's chin. Delilah rewarded her with a rumbling purr. Theresa handed her the animal and led the way to the workbench and storage cabinets. "Over here is where we keep all the tattooing supplies."

"I have my own machine," Cherry said. "A graduation gift from my folks."

Scott joined them. "I hear you're a musician." So much for thinking he was crushed. Theresa should have known better.

Cherry scarcely looked at him. "I'm a music major, yeah."

"I used to play in a band myself." He puffed out his chest.

Theresa figured if she bit down on the inside of her cheek any harder, she'd draw blood. Cherry gave him a scornful look. "I don't play in a *band*. I perform with the school symphony. Cello."

Scott looked so disappointed, Theresa almost felt sorry for him. Almost. "Evenings and weekends, when you'll be working, are our prime time for walk-ins," she said. "They'll keep you busy until you get your own clients." At least she hoped so. With the picketers refusing to give up, walk-in traffic had been slow lately.

"I can do piercings, too," she offered.

"I usually handle the piercings," Scott said.

Cherry shrugged. "I'm just saying I can do them, too."

"I'm sure there won't be a problem dividing up the work." Theresa gave Scott a hard look. *At least there'd better not be.*

He shrugged. "Sure."

He retreated to the front counter, probably to sulk. Theresa guessed she could live with that if it kept him quiet. She turned to Cherry again. "When you get a chance, make some copies of your portfolio so we can display them for the customers."

"Sure thing. And I thought I'd print up some business cards to hand out around campus and stuff—if that's okay with you."

"Of course it's okay. And I'll cover the cost of the

cards." She'd been about to suggest as much, but the girl got ahead of her. She'd have to be on her toes with this kid. "Come on in back and I'll show you where to put your things and we'll go over the operation of the autoclave."

Cherry deposited the cat on the floor and followed Theresa to the storage closet that served as headquarters for the sterilization equipment. "It's the same kind my mom and dad have," she said when Theresa opened the door.

"So I guess you really did grow up in the business," Theresa said, impressed but not wanting to show it too much.

"I started apprenticing when I was a teenager and I'd work summers and holidays for extra money. It's interesting work, but music's really where I want to make my career." Her expression turned sheepish. "I hope it's okay for me to say that. I like to be up-front with people."

"I appreciate that." It was a little scary how together this chick was. Theresa knew there was no way she'd been this calm and confident at Cherry's age. "Why don't we go back up front?"

Scott was still sulking behind the counter. "Why don't you show Cherry how to get into the computer," Theresa said. She turned to Cherry. "We're trying to get all the scheduling and ordering and things like that computerized, but we're not there yet."

She nodded. "My parents are technophobes, too. I keep telling them to join the twenty-first century, but they don't get it."

Now Theresa felt like an Amazon *crone*. She was only seven years older than Elf Girl, but it might as well have been twenty. "Scott's doing a good job of getting us on track," she said. "He can explain the system to you."

"Yeah, sure." He moved over to make room for Cherry in front of the computer.

Ten minutes later, as she was prepping her two o'clock customer—a truck driver named Alan—Theresa congratulated herself on her smooth handling of the potential conflict between Scott and Cherry. The two were both bent over the computer, engrossed in talk of databases, spreadsheets and operating systems.

She'd just started outlining a wolf's head on Alan's ankle when the door bells sounded again and a woman in a pink smock took a hesitant step inside. "Uh, I'm looking for a Miss Theresa Jacobs," she said.

Theresa shut off the tattoo machine. "That's me."

"Oh! Then I do have the right place." Eyes wide, the woman stared around the room.

"Can I help you?" Theresa prompted.

"Oh! Yes. Just a minute. I'll be right back." She exited again, the temple bells jangling in her wake.

"Something tells me she didn't stop by for a tat," the man in the chair said.

"Sorry about the interruption," Theresa apologized.

He shrugged. "I'm not in any hurry."

The woman reappeared in the doorway, her face almost hidden by a large arrangement of yellow roses in a glass vase. "Where should I put these?" she asked.

Theresa's mouth dropped open. After a stunned silence, she managed to speak. "Why are you bringing those in here?"

"You said you were Theresa Jacobs, right?"

She nodded. "Yeah."

"These flowers are for you." She set the arrangement

on the front counter and pointed to the tiny emblem on the left breast pocket of her smock. "From Pecan Street Florists."

"Why is a florist's shop sending me flowers?"

The woman laughed. "Oh, they're not from us. We're just delivering them. There's a card on the arrangement." Her gaze shifted to the man in the chair, and her eyes widened again as she zeroed in on the beginnings of the tattoo there. "I've always wondered—doesn't that hurt?"

"Not much." He grinned. "You ought to try it sometime."

The delivery woman blushed. "I don't think… At least, I never…" She shook her head. "I have to go now. Enjoy your flowers."

When she was gone, they all stared at the roses. There had to be at least a dozen of them, a soft yellow with a blush of pink at the tips of the petals, baby's breath and greenery arranged around them. "They're gorgeous," Cherry said.

"Aren't you going to check the card?" Scott said.

"Maybe later." She switched on the tattoo machine again. In all her twenty-eight years, no one had *ever* sent her flowers. She wasn't sure how to act.

"Oh, go on, check the card," her customer said. "I'm curious now, too."

Reluctantly she shut off the machine and stripped off her gloves, then walked up to the counter.

Up close, the arrangement was even prettier. She wanted to bury her nose amid the buds and see if they smelled like anything. She wanted to feel the petals and see if they were as velvety soft as they looked. But she didn't want to look like a fool in front of everyone, so all she did was reach up and snatch the card from its holder.

The envelope was unsealed, and the card inside was a simple white one. "I'm looking forward to tonight. Kyle."

"Ooooh, you're blushing!" Cherry squealed. She elbowed Scott in the ribs. "It must be good."

"I'll bet it's from that cowboy." Scott leaned over the counter and looked at her around the flowers. "Isn't it?"

"What cowboy?" Cherry asked.

Theresa hated that she was blushing. She wasn't the kind of woman who blushed. But then, she wasn't the kind of woman men sent flowers to, either. She tucked the card inside her top, away from prying eyes. "I suggest we all get back to work," she said and walked briskly back to her customer.

"It is your birthday or something?" he asked.

She shook her head and put on a new pair of gloves. "No, it isn't."

He grinned. "Well, whoever sent you those, I'd say they have good taste."

Because the flowers he'd chosen were so pretty, or because he'd sent them to *her?* She didn't ask. "Why don't you just relax and we'll get started again." She told herself to focus on her work, to stop thinking about the flowers or Kyle Cameron. It was bad enough he'd thrown her for a loop with his kisses. What the hell did he think he was doing turning all romantic and sending her *flowers?*

4

THERESA WAS ALONE IN THE shop when Kyle showed up, just after eleven. He stood on the sidewalk for a minute, watching her through the window as she tidied up around the front counter. She moved with swift efficiency, leaving order in her wake with that knack some women have for setting things to rights with seemingly little effort.

He spotted the roses by the cash register and grinned. She probably hadn't expected those, not after the businesslike way she'd agreed to their "arrangement." But just because they were being practical didn't mean he couldn't throw in a few surprises to keep things interesting.

He made one last check of his reflection in the glass and straightened the bandanna knotted at his neck. Polished boots, creased jeans, starched white shirt and leather vest completed the look, topped by his best Stetson 10X Rancher.

She jumped when the door opened and whirled to face him, a feather duster in one hand. The sight of her in her leather miniskirt and vest with that duster struck him as incongruous. And sexy as hell. Like one of those French maid costumes with a kinky twist. He grinned. "I never was much for housework, but I might be persuaded to help if you promise to tickle me with your feathers there."

She threw the duster at him, hitting him squarely in the chest, and he couldn't help but laugh. Hands on her hips, she looked him up and down, trying for an annoyed expression, but the way her mouth tipped up at the corners and the amusement in her dark eyes gave her away. "I'm done here," she said. "Let me get my purse."

She turned toward the back of the shop, but he snared her with a hand on her arm before she got very far. "How about a proper hello first? After all, we don't have to rush."

"Whatever gave you the idea I was proper?" she purred, but she put her arms around him and gave him a kiss that involved a lot more than just her lips pressed against his. She wrapped herself around him like satin-soft cling wrap. When she pulled away and smiled up at him, it was all he could do to remember to breathe. "I'll be right back," she said and disappeared into the back room.

While he was waiting for her, he walked over to the flowers. Yellow roses because someone had told him yellow flowers were for friendship while red were for love. Besides, they'd looked pretty there in the florist's shop. They looked even better here, arranged in a vase. One of the cats lay beside the vase, watching him, tail twitching. "You leave these alone." Kyle shook a warning finger at the animal. "No snacking."

"I figure you can follow me to my place—" She froze, one hand up in the act of pushing away the beaded curtain that separated the back room from the rest of the shop.

He looked up from the flowers. "I see you got my little present," he said.

He'd expected thanks, praise or maybe even another

kiss. Instead she was frowning. "Why did you pull a stunt like that?" she asked.

"What kind of stunt are you talking about?" He glanced at the roses. "You mean these?"

"I've never been so embarrassed in all my life." She walked behind the counter and began shutting down the computer. "People were asking about them all day. 'Who sent *you* flowers?'" She mimicked a sickly sweet whine. "'Is it your birthday?' I was so tired of it I was ready to throw them in the trash."

He leaned on the counter, reining in his irritation. "And here I thought women liked flowers. That *you'd* like them."

She glanced at him, more doubt than anger in her eyes. "I like flowers all right, but when a man sends a woman flowers, people think it *means* something."

"It's none of their business anyway." He straightened. "I wanted to send flowers to a beautiful woman. So sue me."

She stilled, head down, hair fallen forward hiding her face. He wanted to reach out and tuck those soft locks behind her ear, feel the silk of her hair on his fingers and see if he could read her thoughts in her eyes. "Thanks, but you didn't have to do that," she said after a moment. "It's not like you have to, you know, court me or anything."

He almost laughed at the old-fashioned word. "Oh, I don't know. Don't you think every woman wants a little wooing?" Unable to resist any longer, he did reach forward and tuck her hair behind her ear. It was just as soft as he remembered. He imagined how it would feel wrapped around him and had to back away and shake his head to rid himself of the image. They had a long night ahead. He couldn't let things get out of hand too soon.

He walked her to her car, then trailed her in his truck as she drove to her apartment. When they arrived, he silently followed her up the stairs, enjoying the sway of her hips as she took each step. He took her keys from her and opened the door, heart pounding. *Calm down,* he reminded himself. *This ain't your first rodeo, after all.*

One look at her apartment and he was effectively distracted. It looked like the inside of one of those lingerie shops in the mall—there was pink everywhere, and flowers and lace. Little gold and white knickknacks. Mirrors and paintings in fancy gilt frames. He stared at the leather-clad woman in front of him. "Are we in the right place?" he asked.

"Very funny." She strode past him into the room, flicking on lights. "You want a drink?"

"I'll take a beer if you've got one."

He leaned against the kitchen counter and watched her move about the room. The wallpaper in here was pink pinstripes, and a picture of a kitten in a chef's hat hung over the stove. He nodded to the cat. "You can't blame me for being a little surprised at all this," he said.

She took two beers from the refrigerator and opened them. "At all what?" Amazingly her expression was completely blank.

"This pink, for one thing." He accepted one of the beers and took a long swallow. "You don't look like a pink person."

"So? People aren't always what they seem." She raised the beer to her lips.

He watched the long, smooth column of her throat as she drank. He wanted to kiss every inch of her skin, to feel her pale, slender fingers grip him the way she gripped the beer bottle. He wanted to toss aside the beers and start stripping her naked, but gave himself credit for having more style than that. "Hard day at work?" he asked.

She shrugged. "It was okay, I guess. I hired a new part-timer. A college girl."

"Think she'll work out?"

"Who knows?" She shook her head. "She's kind of scary."

Spoken by a woman who would have a fair amount of men shaking in their boots. "How so?"

"She's just so…sure of herself. Together. Way more than I ever was at her age."

"You seem pretty together now."

"I've learned a few things along the way." She set aside the beer and took two steps toward him. Her breasts brushed the front of his shirt and she reached for the top button.

He covered her hand with his, stopping her. "What are you doing?"

Her lips pursed in a sexy pout. "I figured it's time we get to it."

"No hurry." He left his beer bottle on the counter, then brushed the back of his hand down her cheek. "We ought to spend a little time getting to know each other."

The heavy-lidded look she gave him was guaranteed to make a man's blood boil. Then she slid her hand down between them and squeezed the hard ridge straining his fly. He let out his breath in a rush. "I know all I need to know about you," she said.

Any other time he might have gone for this direct approach but he didn't intend to let her get the upper hand so quickly. He pulled her hand back up to chest level. "Hey, slow down. Don't be so nervous."

"I'm not nervous."

But the flush that bloomed on her cheeks told him otherwise. He smoothed his hand down her hair. "Sure you're nervous. Everybody's nervous the first time."

"You don't look nervous."

"I am, darlin'. I am." He reached around to knead the back of her neck. Her muscles were as tight as guitar strings. "Close your eyes."

She looked wary. "Why?"

"Just close them. When I'm working with a nervous horse, I might blindfold them. It takes away all the distractions, forces them to pay attention just to me."

"I'm not a horse." But she closed her eyes.

"No, ma'am. But you are one fine filly, just the same." He worked his way across her back with his good hand, massaging gently, moving to her shoulders, pausing to plant a kiss in the hollow of her collarbone.

Her eyes flew open. "What are you doing?"

"All right, darlin'. You asked for it." He pulled the bandanna from around his neck.

She stared. "What's that for?"

"I told you, when a horse is too nervous, I blindfold it." He refolded the bandanna, then covered her eyes and awkwardly knotted it, hampered somewhat by the cast on his wrist. He slipped a finger under it to check the fit. "Not too snug, is it?"

She shook her head. "No. What are you going to do?"

He smiled, enjoying the keen edge of desire that knifed through him at the sight of her blindfolded this way. "Trust me, darlin'."

THERESA FOUGHT PANIC, struggling to take deep breaths. Kyle wasn't going to hurt her. And there was something exciting about not being able to see this way. Something incredibly arousing about relying on her other senses to figure out what was going on.

His hand was a little rough, callused but gentle as he stroked her arms. He lifted her hand to his mouth and kissed her palm, the brush of his tongue on her skin sending electric sensations along her nerves.

She took another deep breath, steadying herself, but all she smelled was him. Spicy cologne and masculine sweat—a scent that screamed sex and added fuel to the heat building in her.

He ran his hand across her stomach, pausing to play with the charm in her belly-button ring. "Cute," he said.

"I don't like to think of myself as cute," she said.

"No, you're too tough for that, aren't you?"

She didn't feel very tough now, as he slid his hand up farther to cup the underside of her breast. She gasped, arching toward him.

"Mmm, you do feel good." He lowered the zipper on the front of the vest and pushed aside the two halves of the garment. Cool air rushed across her breasts and her nipples tightened.

He cradled first one breast, then the other, her fullness spilling over his fingers. He trailed his thumb in circles around each breast, each circle smaller than the last, drawing closer but never quite touching the sensitive nipples.

With a strangled cry of frustration, she arched toward him, swaying a little on her high heels.

"Take off your shoes."

She kicked aside the heels.

"Now put your hands on my shoulders."

She did so, wondering what he would do next. She liked foreplay as much as the next gal, but this slow, deliberate exploration was driving her crazy.

He turned his attention to her breasts again, shaping them with his hand, squeezing them. He bent and she felt the hot, wet caress of his tongue and couldn't hold back a moan of pure pleasure as he took her nipple into his mouth.

She leaned into him, gripping his shoulders to keep from sinking to the floor. His mouth was devastatingly thorough, sucking and licking and teasing first one breast and then the other. Every tug of his mouth set up a corresponding tension in her womb. She was wet and swollen and had to clamp her mouth shut to keep from begging him to satisfy her.

He smoothed his hand up her thigh, all the way to her waist, where he grasped the elastic of her tights and pulled. "Let's get you out of these, all right?"

She couldn't shed the hose fast enough, supporting herself with one hand on his shoulder while he helped her divest herself of them. Her skirt followed shortly, and her panties, leaving her naked.

She cursed the blindfold that kept her from seeing his expression. He was silent for a couple of minutes, and she knew he was studying her. She hugged her arms across her chest and scowled at him. "What is it? Never saw a tattooed woman before?"

"Not one with such a lovely canvas to work on." He pulled her arms away, coaxing them around him once more, then hugged her closer still, his cast braced at her back, his free hand reaching down between them to cover her crotch. "You are ready for me, aren't you?" he whispered, his tongue in her ear as his fingers slid into her.

She thrust against him hard, unable to hold back. Her body wasn't paying any attention to her mind anymore. She'd been reduced to this all-consuming need. A moment longer and she was sure her legs wouldn't be able to support her anymore. She'd be melted from the inside out.

And then she was swept up into his arms and he was carrying her across the room. "Where's the bedroom?" he asked.

"First door on the right."

She braced herself for a rough landing on the bed, but he managed to lay her down gently, the cast scraping a little at her back. For a pretty average-size guy, he was strong. Everywhere she laid her hand, she met with hard muscle, the kind that didn't come from spending days in the gym.

He moved away, and without his warmth she felt cold. "What are you doing?" she asked.

"I thought you might be tired of being the only one naked."

Then he was beside her in the bed, his body covering hers. She reached out and felt one shoulder and the back of his head. She closed her eyes behind the blindfold and tried to take in everything her other senses were telling her: the salty taste of his skin when she ran her tongue along his jaw, the rough hairs on his calf as he knelt beside her, the iron heat of his erection nudging against her thigh. She reached down and felt him twitch in her hand. She smiled. She wasn't the only one ready for him to be inside her.

"There are condoms in the drawer of the bedside table," she said.

"Don't you worry, darlin'. I came prepared." He slid down her body, nudging her thighs farther apart.

She clutched at his head, his hair brushing softly against the tips of her fingers. "Stop calling me that. I'm not your darling."

"All right then. The-ree-ssaa." He drew the name out in a husky drawl, the last syllable breathed out like a sigh, the air rushing over her clit in a too-soft caress.

She arched toward him until his mouth covered her and his tongue began to stroke. She clutched at the sheets, the need inside her coiling even tighter. She smiled, knowing the rush she craved wasn't far away.

She forgot everything then—the blindfold and the bed and the man. All her senses zeroed in on her own skin and bones and the delicious heat building in waves within her, washing over and through her.

She held nothing back, and when she came, she screamed. The sound echoed around them, a shout of triumph and release and pure joy. As it faded away, she became aware of his labored breathing and the steady pounding of her heart. She kept her eyes shut tight, unwilling to leave this dreamlike state where everything seemed so perfect.

At that instant, she forgave Kyle the flowers and the romance and everything that hinted at him trying to make her into something she was not. She forgave him and welcomed him and wanted him all over again. She caressed the solid bulk of his shoulders and inhaled deeply of his musky scent, smiling to herself. A man who could make her feel this wonderful was worth keeping around awhile longer.

KYLE WATCHED THE LAST contractions of her climax move through her, admiring the flush that crept across her breasts and up her neck. He breathed in the womanly scent of her, every breath making his cock twitch. Sitting back on his heels, he slipped on the condom, then reached for her again. He wanted to be inside her before she was all the way back to earth, to feel her contract around him with the remnants of her own release.

As soon as he was all the way inside, he reached up and pulled off the blindfold and tossed it aside. She blinked at him, then smiled, a sated look in her eyes that made him want her even more. "Hi," she whispered.

"Hello." He emphasized the greeting with a hard thrust.

Her eyes widened and she raised up on her elbows, watching as he began to move in and out. "Do I pass inspection?" he asked, a little unnerved by the way she fixed her gaze on him. Like most men, he was somewhat preoccupied by this particular anatomical feature, particularly at moments like this. But it was after all a penis—not a body part that would ever win awards for beauty.

"Oh, yes. I think you'll do just fine." She lay back again and slid her hands under her ass, lifting herself to a more acute angle, one that made her tighten around him more, so that his vision lost focus and his breath came in gasps.

"You like that?" she asked, as she squeezed him tighter still, then released.

His reply was a muffled grunt. He lowered his head and focused on the task at hand, aware of her soft inner thighs brushing against him, her sweet musky scent surrounding him.

He came hard, bucking against her, reaching out to grasp her hips, sinking his fingers into her soft flesh as he spent himself in her. He sank onto her, head on her chest, arms surrounding her in a hug. Some dimly heard portion of his brain told him he must be crushing her, but he paid no heed. He wanted her close to him in this moment. As close as she could be.

He didn't know how long they lay together like that before she prodded his shoulder. "Roll over," she ordered.

He complied, sliding out of her. Eyes still shut, he stripped off the condom, then realized he had no idea where to put it. "There's a trash can in the bathroom," she said.

He nodded. "Bathroom." He wasn't sure he had the strength to roll over now, much less propel himself upright and to the bathroom.

She took the condom from him and he opened his eyes in time to see her walking toward the bathroom, hips swaying, that gorgeous fall of black hair swinging in time to her movements. He closed his eyes again, smiling. Did he know how to pick them or what?

5

THERESA WOKE THE NEXT MORNING with the drowsy, sated feeling of having been thoroughly satisfied. She smiled at the memory of the previous night's lovemaking. Her instincts about Kyle hadn't been wrong; the man definitely knew what was what in the bedroom.

She extended her arms over her head and pointed her toes in a long cat stretch, letting her body waken gradually to the softness of rumpled sheets, the diffused sunlight streaming around the edge of the blinds and the tantalizing aroma of fresh-brewed coffee.

She heard the squeak of door hinges and opened her eyes to see Kyle walking toward her. He had the fingers of his good hand looped through two mugs of coffee, a plate of toast balanced precariously on top. "Mornin', sleepyhead," he drawled.

The drawl and the smile that accompanied it sent a tickle of arousal through her middle. Or maybe it was the sight of him dressed only in jeans, the top button undone, bare feet peeking out from the hem. Since when had bare toes been sexy to her? Not to mention those killer abs and heart-stopping chest. How did a cowboy get to be so damned good-looking?

She sat up, tucking the sheet up under her arms.

"Ready for a little breakfast?" He set his burden on the nightstand and handed her a mug of steaming coffee. He leaned over and kissed her forehead, an unexpected, sweet gesture.

She wrapped both hands around the mug and drank deeply. She'd never had a man bring her breakfast before. Sexy and macho she could handle. Sweet made her uneasy. "What's with all this?" she asked, gesturing at the toast.

He pulled a napkin from the pocket of his jeans and handed it to her, along with a piece of toast. "I woke up and was hungry. Figured you might be, too. After all, we worked up quite an appetite last night." His grin reduced her insides to mush.

She nibbled toast, watching him out of the corner of her eye. Despite their rather strenuous night and the early hour, he radiated vitality and sex appeal. She debated shoving aside the food and attacking him.

"What are you staring at?" He brushed crumbs from his hands.

She shifted her eyes away from him, pretending great interest in the remaining toast. "What makes you think I was staring?"

"I saw you." He crooked his arm and flexed his muscles. "You were staring at me."

Busted. She chewed the last of the toast and swallowed. "I was just wondering if you spend all day in a gym."

He grinned, obviously pleased. Score one for the male ego. "Nah. I work out sometimes, but mostly it's just the work I do. It takes a lot of muscle to throw a calf around."

She arranged herself more comfortably, folding her legs.

"What exactly is it you do in the rodeo? I mean, what does calf roping involve?"

It was his turn to stare. "You live in Texas and you don't know what goes on at a rodeo?"

"Hey, it's not my scene."

"I thought everybody had been to the rodeo at least once."

She shrugged. "I went when I was a kid. One of those things where the Lions Club or some group like that gets free tickets to take a bunch of underprivileged kids."

She waited for him to ask if she was underprivileged and how, but thankfully, he didn't. He set aside the plate and scooted over closer to her. "Okay, well here's how it works. The roper—that's me—is mounted and waits until the calf is released from the chute. When the calf reaches a certain point in the arena, the barrier on the box I'm in drops, and I take off after the calf. The idea, really, is for me and the calf to hit that barrier at the exact same time. Too soon and I get a ten-second penalty, too late and I'm eating up time on the clock."

"So far, the calf's doing all the work," she teased.

"You just listen. I'm getting to my part. As soon as I get my lasso around the calf, my horse stops, then I dismount, run to the calf, throw it over on its side—that's called *flanking*—and tie three of its legs together with the pigging string. That's a short loop of rope I've had clenched in my teeth all this time. And while I'm doing this, my horse is keeping the rope taut. When I've got the calf tied, I throw my hands up to signal to the judges that I'm done, then I get back on the horse and ride forward a little to put some slack in the rope. The calf has to stay tied for at least six seconds after that or no score. The cowboy with the fastest time wins."

"How long does all this take?"

"The record is a little over seven seconds. Between eight and nine seconds is considered really good."

She leaned back against the pillows, trying to imagine the action he'd described. "Okay, I'm a little impressed. But the next question is—why? It doesn't sound like much fun for you or the calf."

"On the ranch you have to tie the calves for branding and cutting them. That's castrating them, for you city girls."

She punched his shoulder. "I know what it is. So how long have you been doing this?"

"Ten years. I used to be in the top ten or fifteen, but lately I've been slipping. Younger guys, seventeen, eighteen, nineteen—they're faster."

He frowned, tiny lines fanning out from the corners of his eyes. How was it wrinkles could look so awful on a woman and so sexy on a man like Kyle? "How old are you?" she asked.

"Twenty-nine and holding." He put his arm around her and pulled her close. "How old are you?"

"Twenty-eight." They were both creeping up on thirty and what did they have to show for themselves? It was a scary thought.

As if reading her mind, he said, "My sister, Kristen, keeps telling me I need to decide what I'm going to do with the rest of my life."

She leaned her head on his shoulder, enjoying the warm, solid feel of him. "What do you want to do?"

He sighed. "I don't know. But it's not staying home on the ranch like she wants."

The dissatisfaction in his voice surprised her. She raised

her head to look into his eyes. "Didn't you tell me your family had been ranching forever? And isn't that what cowboys do?"

His eyes met hers, his expression troubled. "I'll let you in on a secret. I was raised in the saddle, but that don't mean I want to spend the rest of my life there."

"I don't understand. Didn't you just tell me you've spent ten years on the rodeo circuit?"

He drew up his legs and rested his wrists on his knees. "It's complicated. Or maybe it's just real simple. I started rodeoing because I was good at it and I liked it well enough and most of all because it got me off the ranch. I got to travel, make some money." He shrugged. "When you think about it, except for the traveling, which can get to be a drag, there's not a hell of a lot of real work involved. You show up and compete, then head on down the road to the next show."

"Are you admitting you're lazy?" Running her hand up his arm, feeling the hard ridges of muscle, she didn't really believe that.

He grinned. "Not lazy. Just unmotivated. Ranching's hard, dirty work and it's about as exciting as watching the grass grow. Not to mention the rotten hours and the lack of outside entertainment."

"I'm sure I'd hate it."

He shook his head. "Kristen and her husband love it, but she doesn't understand it's not what I want to do."

"So what do you want to do?"

He turned toward her. "Right now, I want to make love to a certain gorgeous woman." He pulled back the sheet and bent to nibble along her collarbone.

She recognized a change of subject, but decided not to push it. It wasn't any of her business anyway. She put both arms around him and arched her body to his. "You ready to do a different kind of riding, cowboy?" she purred.

"Maybe you should be the one to ride this time, while I take it easy."

"I'll show you *easy*." She bit his shoulder hard enough to get his attention. "Come on, cowboy, show me your stuff."

Laughing, they rolled across the bed in each other's arms. Theresa deliberately put the seriousness of the moment before aside. Right now, she and Kyle were just passing time with each other, enjoying a pleasant interlude before they had to get on with the rest of their lives.

IT WAS ALMOST LUNCHTIME before Kyle and Theresa finally made it out of bed. His idea of a morning well spent, he thought as he drove across town toward his orthopedic surgeon's office. He hadn't had much trouble talking Theresa into seeing him tonight, either. If he worked it right, he could probably convince her to let him stay with her once his friend A.J. returned from his hitch on the rigs. With any luck, he'd avoid returning to the ranch until it was time to hit the circuit again.

There was no lineup of patients at the surgeon's office, so Kyle was shown right in.

Dr. Hank Gunderson examined the injured wrist. "Is it giving you any pain?" he asked.

"Nah." Kyle shifted on the table. "Itches like hell sometimes, though."

Dr. Gunderson clipped the gauze into place. "X-rays

show it's healing fine. Of course, you can't expect to mend quite as quickly as you did a few years ago, when you broke your collarbone— Wasn't that it?"

He groaned, remembering. "That calf kicked me into next month." He frowned at his unwrapped arm. After only a little over a week in the cast, it seemed smaller and weaker. "How soon can I lose the cast? It's getting to be a pain." Not to mention it was seriously cramping his style with a certain gorgeous brunette. He couldn't wait to put *both* arms all the way around her without that chunk of fiberglass in the way.

"If you promise to be careful, you can probably get by with taping it and wearing an air cast. You can take that off when you shower, but you'll want to leave it on most of the time."

"Great."

Dr. Gunderson turned to a supply cabinet and took out a package of elastic gauze and a white cardboard box. "So what have you been doing with yourself now that you're off the circuit for a while?"

"Not much." He held out his arm and Dr. Gunderson wrapped it with tape. "Kicking around, trying to stay out of trouble."

Dr. Gunderson slipped on the air cast and showed him how to adjust the Velcro straps. "Unless you have problems, I don't need to see you again for another five weeks. You should be fully healed by then. But I'll want you to keep the wrist taped when you compete and work with the Justin Healers on some therapy."

He nodded. The Justin Healers were the medics of the rodeo, many of them former rodeo riders themselves. "Thanks, Doc."

He was settling his bill when someone behind him said, "Kyle Cameron, is that you?"

He turned and saw a lanky man in jeans and a T-shirt standing next to a small boy whose arm was in a sling. Recognition clicked in his brain. "Brady Robbins, you old son of a gun!"

He hugged his friend. Back in his late teens and early twenties, he and Brady had been running buddies, traveling the rodeo circuit together, splitting expenses and competing against each other in calf roping. But Brady had left the circuit years ago to take a job at the family hardware store.

"Who is this?" Kyle stepped back and grinned at the kid. As if he didn't recognize the spitting image of Brady, right down to the cowlick sticking up at the back of his head.

"This is my boy, Derrick." Brady put his arm around the kid, who stood up a little straighter and grinned, showing one tooth missing. "He had a little mishap at a mutton bustin'."

Mutton bustin' was a popular event at rodeos. Any child could enter and attempt to catch and ride one of the sheep turned loose in the arena. "You going to be a rodeo cowboy like your dad?" Kyle asked.

The boy hooked the thumb of his good hand into his belt loop and puffed out his chest. "I'm gonna be even *better'n* my dad."

They laughed. Brady nodded at the cast on Kyle's arm. "What happened to you?"

"I was in a rodeo over in Stephenville and an ornery calf got the better of me."

Brady shook his head. "So you're still ridin' the circuit?"

"Yeah. Guess I'm not smart enough to quit. What about you? You still in the hardware business?"

He shook his head. "They built a big new Wal-Mart down the road, put us out of business. Now I'm working construction, building homes in one of those new subdivisions west of here."

"It must suit you. You look good." He'd put on a little weight, but just enough to make him look more solid. Settled.

Brady grinned. "I can't believe you're still rodeoin'. So I guess this means you aren't married."

He shook his head. "I haven't let a woman lasso me yet."

A nurse appeared in the waiting-room doorway. "Derrick Robbins?"

"Looks like we got to go." Brady stuck out his hand. "Good to see you, man. Good luck with the wrist."

"Good to see you, too."

Kyle rode an otherwise empty elevator down to street level, trying to wrap his mind around the idea of his old buddy Brady as a dad with a kid old enough to be in school. Not that he didn't know a lot of men his age with families, but none of those men had ever been like him, living the free and easy life, competing for big money, their days and nights revolving around those few minutes in the arena and celebrating or commiserating at the beer halls afterward. That kind of life seemed a long way from where Brady was now.

If he'd thought Brady would envy his freedom, he hadn't seen any sign of it. If anything, his old pard had looked a little sorry for Kyle. *Almost thirty and still playing a kid's game,* he imagined Brady saying to his wife. *Who does he think he's fooling?*

He studied his reflection in the polished metal doors of

the elevator. Except for the cast, he looked the same as he always had. A few more lines around his eyes maybe, but he was as lean and muscular as ever, his hair just as thick. He hadn't really changed on the outside.

He exited the elevator and headed for his truck. He'd be lying to himself if he said he hadn't grown up and changed on the inside. He was getting tired of his life—of the travel, of trying to keep up with young hotshots barely out of their teens, of not knowing where he'd be or what he'd be doing next year or even next month.

He didn't want to settle down on the ranch and take up the kind of life Kristen wanted for him, but he couldn't see keeping on the way he had been, either. There had to be a compromise somewhere, something he could do that would be satisfying and productive without being boring.

He started up the truck and waited for traffic to clear before he turned out into the street. At least he had tonight to look forward to. Theresa was anything but boring, and she didn't badger a man with questions. Maybe because she didn't want him poking too deep into her own affairs.

He remembered her remark about attending the rodeo as part of some charity group of underprivileged kids. He'd about bit his tongue off to keep from asking about that. After all, they'd made a bargain. They weren't going to concern themselves with the past or future. All they would focus on was right now and enjoying themselves with each other. Things didn't get complicated that way. Heaven knows, he wasn't a man who liked complications.

THERESA HAD SPENT SO MUCH time saying goodbye to Kyle, she was late to work. Not that it really mattered, since

Scott had a key, but she hated having to rush. So she wasn't in the best of moods when she was confronted with yet another group of protesters. Today the crowd was all women, some with little kids in tow. *Great*, she thought. *Teach your babies to be intolerant from the start.*

She started to say as much when one of the women reached down to jerk her kid out of Theresa's path, as if she were afraid the slightest contact with the owner of a den of iniquity might prove fatal. Theresa managed a smarmy smile. "Don't worry, hon," she said in a butter-wouldn't-melt-in-my-mouth drawl. "I don't have cooties or anything."

The horrified expression on the woman's face should have made her laugh, but she couldn't muster anything stronger than disgust. She shoved open the door to the shop and slammed it behind her.

"I ought to be able to swear out a warrant against those people for something," she grumbled as she stashed her purse behind the counter. "Harassment or stupidity or something."

Scott and Cherry scarcely noticed her. They were standing in the middle of the shop, a large music case between them. "It's about time you got here," Scott said. "I've been trying to tell Cherry she can't bring this thing in here."

"It's not a thing, it's a cello!" Cherry whirled to face Theresa. "I thought I could practice during slow spells. The customers might even like the music."

Scott's look was scornful. "This is a tattoo shop. Our customers like rock and roll. Not cello music."

"How do you know? Have you asked them?"

"Both of you, quiet!" Theresa squeezed her head between her hands, trying to drive out the headache already throbbing there. "Cherry, put the cello in the back. We'll decide later if you can play it or not."

Cherry stuck her tongue out at Scott, then lugged the case toward the back. Theresa turned to him. "I need you to close tonight," she said.

He shoved his hands in the pockets of his cargo shorts. "I was sort of planning on going out."

"You can go out after you close up here. There'll still be plenty of women in the bars."

"C'mon! You make it sound like I go around picking up anything in a skirt."

She arched one eyebrow. "You're the one who's always bragging about your conquests."

He glanced toward the back room. "Not so loud, okay?"

"You worried she'll think you're a tomcat?" Stud Boy's discomfort was too delicious not to savor, but she did lower her voice. "I thought you enjoyed that reputation." Especially since she suspected he exaggerated his conquests.

"You kidding?" He made a show of polishing his nails on his shirt front. "I know dudes who would kill for a rep like mine. But I don't want to scare her off by revealing too much too soon, you know?"

"So see, it will be good for you to stay in and work one night."

"Why can't you close tonight?" He followed her to the front counter and watched her log on to the computer.

"I'm going out." Actually her plans called for staying in with a certain cowboy, but Scott didn't need to know that.

"You mean you have a date?" He shook his head. "You never date."

She glared at him. "Just because I don't feel the need to

announce the details of my social life to everyone who walks through the door doesn't mean I don't have one."

"You can't keep a secret like that. Not in a place like this." He shrugged. "Besides, everybody knows you don't date."

She gave him her best go-to-hell glare, a look that had reduced lesser men to stammering idiots. "Do I look like a nun to you?"

He held up both hands and took a step back. "I'm just saying…"

Cherry emerged from the back room and joined them. Today she was wearing ripped jeans and a tie-dyed tank top that showed off her tattoos and her not inconsiderable cleavage. Theresa almost felt sorry for Scott, who had trouble keeping his eyes off his new co-worker. "I got an appointment coming in at two and a class at four-thirty," she said.

Theresa nodded. "That should be okay. I'll be here until six or so. Scott's going to close."

"I can come back at seven and work till close." Cherry turned to Scott. "Friday night's liable to be busy, right?"

He slouched against the counter. "Nothing I can't handle."

"No, that's a good idea," Theresa said. "The two of you can watch each other's backs."

"Whatever." Scott's bored expression was entirely too studied. And the way his eyes kept darting to Cherry completely gave him away. To Theresa's surprise, Cherry was casting a few sly looks of her own.

Well, well, well. Maybe there was some spark between those two….

The bells on the door jangled and she turned, expecting to greet a customer. Instead she found one of her favorite people, Madeline Cupples, who owned the Excessories Boutique down the street.

The petite, white-haired woman with a single diamond in the side of her nose held up her arms and enveloped the much taller, younger woman in an embrace. "Theresa, *chica!* You're just who I wanted to see."

"Hello, Madeline." Theresa smiled at her friend. "How are you doing?"

"I'm hanging in there. That's the best that can be expected these days."

"What can I do for you? You ready for another piercing? Or maybe another tattoo to go with the rosebud I did for you last year?"

The older woman grinned. "Maybe later. Right now, I wanted to tell you what's going on on the street."

Theresa led her friend over to a pair of folding chairs and they sat. "Not more bad news, I hope," she said.

"No, this is good news. The local business owners are banding together to get rid of the mud Carter and his cronies are slinging at us. And we want you to join us."

Theresa made a face. The idea of endless meetings, even with people who were mostly her friends, didn't appeal to her. "Do you really think it will do any good?"

"We can't just sit here like lumps and let *them* do all the talking, can we?"

Theresa shook her head. "I wish you luck, but that's not really my kind of thing. I'm thinking if we ignore all this, it will die down after the election."

"Or maybe not, if Carter wins."

Could that happen? Would people really vote for a blowhard like Carter, who was trying to do away with what was after all an Austin institution? She shook her head. "Thanks for asking me, though."

Madeline patted Theresa's knee, then stood. "You think about it. We'd love to have you working with us anytime."

Theresa stayed seated and watched Madeline bounce out of the shop. Where did the older woman get all her energy? Between trying to sort out her employees' love lives *and* deal with protesters *and* run a business, Theresa was exhausted. She was doubly glad she'd let Kyle talk her into getting away with him tonight. Things with him were uncomplicated. So far, he'd been the rare man who didn't ask a lot of questions or expect her to be anything other than herself.

She wasn't optimistic that attitude would last, but then, it didn't have to. They were in this for the short haul, for a vacation from the other problems in their lives. She only wished she'd thought of a similar arrangement sooner.

6

THERESA GOT BACK TO HER apartment a little after six o'clock and changed her jeans and halter for a pair of form-fitting leather pants and a red satin bustier. She nodded approvingly at her reflection in the bedroom mirror. This was an outfit guaranteed to keep a man off guard. And Kyle deserved to be a little more unsettled around her, especially after the way he'd shaken her up last night.

She still couldn't believe she'd actually let him blindfold her. And that she'd enjoyed it. She rubbed her hand across her stomach, trying to ignore the nervous shimmy that ran through her at the memory. Okay, so the cowboy was dynamite in the sack. No problem with that. None at all. It didn't mean anything in particular that he rocked her world the way no one ever had.

Besides, that was probably just because it had been their first night together. All that anticipation and the excitement of being with someone new probably combined to make things a little more erotic than they would have been otherwise. Things would probably be downhill from here on out.

She turned away from the mirror and began to rummage through her jewelry box. She hoped the sex didn't get dull too soon. She still had—what?—almost five weeks to enjoy her cowboy. She wanted to make the best of them.

When the doorbell rang, she took her time answering it. It wouldn't do to let him think she was too eager. But her cool facade slipped a little when she opened the door and saw him standing there. The casual cowboy had been replaced by a dangerously sexy man in tight black jeans and polished black boots, black tab-collar shirt and a black Stetson tilted low over his eyes. She put her hand to her chest, as if to hide the furious pounding of her heart.

He let out a low whistle. "If all the angels looked like you, every man would get religion." One step across the threshold and he was pulling her close, his mouth covering hers in a warm, welcoming kiss.

Trying to stay in charge of things—though part of her voted for ripping his clothes off then and there—she pushed away and took two steps back. "You certainly are dressed up," she said.

He glanced down at his outfit. "I've been told I clean up all right. Besides, I have to keep up with you."

She turned her back to him and strolled toward the kitchen. "Can I get you a drink?"

"That's okay. We'd better leave or we'll be late."

That stopped her. She faced him once more. "Late for what?"

"We have dinner reservations."

"Dinner?" The sudden hollowness in her stomach had nothing to do with hunger. "You never said anything about dinner."

In three strides, he closed the gap between them and took her hand. "I believe I promised you something better than leftover bar pizza." He stroked his thumb across her knuckles. "And I'd never disappoint a lady."

"No one ever said I was a lady." She'd long ago stopped expecting them to. She wasn't one of those delicate ultra-feminine types men fawned over. Who wanted a fawning man, anyway?

He closed his hand around her fingers. "Come on, you'll enjoy this." He tugged her toward the door.

Still uncertain of the wisdom of going along with his plans, she snagged her purse from the table by the door and allowed him to lead her to his truck. "You didn't have to do this," she grumbled as he opened the passenger door for her. "It's not like we're really dating or anything."

"We both have to eat," he answered a moment later, as he slid into the driver's seat. He checked the mirrors, then started the engine. "Besides, you want to keep your strength up—for later."

His grin was an exaggerated leer. She couldn't help but laugh, even as desire fluttered in her middle. She fastened her seat belt and settled back in the seat. "I am a little hungry." She slicked her tongue across her lips, making sure he noticed.

He shifted in his seat and she allowed herself a smug smile. Oh, he'd noticed all right.

He drove toward Town Lake and pulled into the parking lot of the Hyatt. At first she thought they were going to the Foothills Restaurant, famous for its fajitas and its view of the lake. But he cruised past the hotel and parked in the shade of a live oak tree, next to a boat landing. "Ever been on a dinner cruise?" he asked as he set the parking brake and unfastened his seat belt.

She stared at the double-decker boat tricked out like a paddle wheeler, minus the paddle wheel. *Lone Star,* proclaimed the lettering on the prow. The American and Texas flags snapped in the evening breeze off the stern.

Kyle came around and opened her door and took her hand to help her out. This flustered her even more. She hadn't expected him to wait on her like this; she'd just been too stunned to move.

They made their way across the dock and up the gangplank to the boat, where a blue-coated waiter/sailor led them to a table on the lower deck along the railing. From here, they had a prime view of the lake and the city skyline around it. "Have you done this before?" she asked as Kyle sat across from her.

He shook his head. "No, but I've always wanted to."

She arranged her napkin in her lap and fiddled with her silverware, avoiding looking at him directly, but unable to keep from sneaking peeks out of the corner of her eye. Every time she saw him, she ended up like this—unsure of herself, not knowing what to expect next.

That first day he'd come into the shop, she'd thought she had him all figured out. He was a sexy cowboy out for a good time. Someone who, in return, would show her a good time in the process. But then he kept revealing new sides of his personality, aspects that didn't fit the image she'd put together in her mind.

Cowboys were supposed to be taciturn chauvinists or opinionated rednecks. Sexy, sure. Maybe a little wild and fun to be with. But not smooth and sophisticated, smart and considerate.

With a lurch, the boat pulled away from the dock. Soft

music swelled over the throb of the engines, and a waiter brought a bottle of wine to the table and poured them each a glass. She sipped, hardly tasting the beverage.

He reached across the table and squeezed her hand. "Come on, relax. We're supposed to be having fun here, remember?"

She nodded and smoothed her fingers along the edge of the linen-draped table. "I guess I'm just not used to this kind of treatment."

"What kind of treatment is that?"

"You know. All...this." She gestured toward the plush interior of the boat, with its candlelit tables filled with well-dressed couples.

He frowned. "The men you usually date don't take you to nice places?"

She moved her fork a half inch to the left. "The men I usually go out with are more the beer-and-burgers type." She straightened and met his gaze. "I guess I'm a beer-and-burgers type of woman, too."

He shook his head. "No. I think you might have grown used to beer and burgers, but that doesn't mean you don't think about better things sometimes." He squeezed her hand. "It doesn't mean you don't deserve to be treated like a queen."

His voice was low, soft as a caress, the words seeping into her like warm water flooding through cracks in a wall. If she listened to him long enough, she'd forget what they were really up to here.

The waiter arrived to take their order, breaking the spell, and she pulled her hand away and fussed with her napkin in her lap. By the time they'd made their choices and were alone again, she'd composed herself enough to strike a casual pose and smile seductively across the table. "I'm glad you've figured out that I deserve to be treated like royalty. I find I get along so much better with a man once he's learned that."

He laughed and raised his wineglass. "To the queen. And her loyal subject."

They touched glasses and drank and she began to feel a little better. What had she been worried about, anyway? It wasn't as if Kyle had some ulterior motive. He'd made it clear from the start what he was after; he just had a different idea of foreplay than most of the men she'd met.

"Hey, your cast is different." She nodded to the plastic contraption around his arm that had replaced the gauze-wrapped fiberglass.

"It's an air cast." He winked at her, a slow, sexy lowering of his eyelid that made her catch her breath. "It comes off when I want to take a shower—or *other* things."

She took another drink of wine, trying to calm the flutter in her stomach as she thought of those "other things."

"Ladies and gentlemen, if I could direct your attention to the Congress Avenue Bridge just ahead, we've come to one of the highlights of the evening." The voice over the PA interrupted her reverie. "The largest urban colony of Mexican free-tailed bats is about to set out for its nightly foraging. As many as seven-hundred-and-fifty-thousand bats live in the expansion joints of the bridge. Nightly the colony consumes ten-thousand to thirty-thousand pounds of insects."

"Only a Texan would make a tourist attraction out of a flying rodent," Kyle observed as he scooted his chair closer to Theresa.

"Hush. It's interesting." As the announcer reeled off a few more facts about the bats, small, dark figures began to flit from beneath the bridge. Within another minute, a black cloud of bats rose up, the sound of their wings merging into a throbbing like a thousand heartbeats. The cloud spread out over the water, passing over the boat and dispersing.

"I guess we have the bats to thank that we're not plagued by mosquitoes," Kyle said as the waiter delivered their first course. "One more thing to love about Austin."

"It's a great city," she said as she dipped a chilled shrimp in cocktail sauce. "But then, I've never lived in any others, so I can't compare."

"You've always lived in Austin?"

She nodded. "I was born and raised here."

"Ever think about living somewhere else?"

She shrugged. "Not really." Austin was home, or as close to it as she knew. The thought of going away had never appealed to her.

While savoring the best shrimp cocktail she'd ever had, she turned her chair more toward the railing, feasting on scenery every bit as fine as the food. The boat glided past parks and posh hotels, drawing stares and waves from tourists and locals on the hike-and-bike path around the lake. Ducks swam alongside, obviously hoping for a handout, while a trio of elegant swans remained aloof. A racing scull manned by four women slid by like a giant water bug, and two kids in a canoe pantomimed lassoing the bigger boat and going for a free ride.

When the waiter set their steaks in front of them, Theresa turned her chair to the table once more. "This looks amazing," she said, slicing into the tender meat.

"Better than leftover bar pizza?"

She laughed. "Definitely." She popped a bite of steak into her mouth and chewed, eyes closed, a moan of pure pleasure escaping her.

"It's the bourbon-mushroom sauce," he said. "I heard it's the chef's own secret recipe."

She looked at him, then burst out laughing again.

"What?" He drew back, feigning offense. "What's so funny?"

"You!" She took a drink of wine and tried to catch her breath. "Since when does a rodeo cowboy know anything about bourbon-mushroom sauce? Or wine?" She looked at her glass. "It's very good, by the way."

He sat back in his chair. "I have a confession to make."

She pulled her chair up closer to the table and sat up straighter. "This I've got to hear."

He held up his wineglass, apparently studying the scenery through the prism of crystal and red wine. "When I was in high school, I went through what I guess you'd call a preppy phase. I read up on wine and art and food and wore button-down shirts and was pretty much insufferable."

She tried to picture this paragon of western manhood as a buttoned-up snob, but the resulting image gave her the giggles. "Why would you do something like that?"

He shrugged. "Why else? I was rebelling against my parents. They were ranchers who lived for starched Wranglers, pickup trucks and chicken-fried steak. I had to do something completely different."

Her giggles subsided and she took a long drink of water. "In a kind of crazy way, that makes sense."

"All kids rebel against their parents at some point, don't

they?" He leaned toward her. "I've made my confession. Now it's your turn. What did you do to rebel?" He gestured toward her with his fork. "Is the tattoo thing part of it that stuck?"

"Not exactly." She traced a drop of moisture down the side of her water glass and looked out over the water. The setting sun painted the white limestone cliffs on the opposite shore in sherbet hues. It's not that she felt the need to hide her past from anyone, it was just that the story was so damned awkward to tell without having to deal with sticky emotions like disgust and pity.

"Hey, you don't have to tell me if you don't want to," he said. "I didn't mean to go sticking my nose in your personal business."

"No, it's okay." She spread her hands flat on the table, amazed at how calm she was. How perfectly natural it felt to tell Kyle things about herself she seldom mentioned. "My real parents were out of the picture pretty early on. My dad skipped out when I was a baby and my mom had problems with drinking and drugs, so my brother Zach and I ended up in foster homes."

"So how was that?" No pity in his voice or on his face. Not yet, anyway.

"Most of the time, it pretty much sucked. I ran away when I was fourteen. And when I was fifteen. And sixteen. The last time I stayed out on the street maybe six months." She frowned. Those dark times were a blur now: sleeping in abandoned buildings, begging for change, scoring drugs. Just as well she didn't remember more, or she might be more ashamed. As it was, it was just another part of who she was. Nothing to be proud of but nothing she could change, either. "I was hanging out with the wrong crowd, doing drugs and other stuff that wasn't good."

"Makes my attempts at acting out seem pretty ridiculous," he said.

She smiled. "I never do anything halfway."

He took another drink and studied her over the rim of his glass. "So what happened?"

"My brother came and got me one day and told me to stop trying to kill myself or he'd make me *wish* I was dead. He moved me in with him, made me go back to school and generally stayed on my case every day."

"I bet you hated that."

She nodded. "I did. But I loved him. And I knew he loved me." She reached for her own glass to chase down the lump that had suddenly risen in her throat. All that had happened so long ago; it surprised her that she could still be so emotional about it.

Kyle's hand covered hers. "I'd like to meet this brother of yours someday."

She nodded. "Zach's pretty special."

"I guess you miss him, now that he's— Where did you say? Chicago?"

She nodded again, swallowing another lump of tears. "Yeah, but from what I hear, he's having a blast. Learning about art and being in love and all."

He stared out over the water, his face solemn. "So you're here carrying on the family business, so to speak, while I'm doing everything I can to stay away from the business my own family's built up over the years." He glanced at her. "I must seem pretty stupid to you."

"No." She shook her head. "I don't think that at all."

He rubbed the back of his neck. "I don't know. Maybe I am stupid. It's not like I don't know all about ranching, or like I don't have any talent for it."

"Actually I think it takes a special kind of bravery to walk away from what everyone else thinks is good but what you know in your heart isn't right for you."

Their eyes met, and for an instant the independence she'd clung to so fiercely for so long receded and she gave in to a seldom-acknowledged fantasy of belonging to someone. Crazy as it sounded, she and this cowboy had made a connection that went beyond a physical joining. For the first time ever, she felt as if someone understood her and knew what she was feeling.

Then the waiter arrived to pour more wine and the spell was broken. Kyle focused on his steak again and she stared out over the railing, glad of the dim light to hide the sudden flush that warmed her face. Obviously she'd had too much to drink if she was having crazy thoughts like that. The only thing she and Kyle shared was physical attraction. Anything else was pure imagination on her part.

When dinner was over, Kyle paid the check and they walked back out to his truck. She assumed they'd head back to her apartment now, but instead he headed out to Highway 2222, the winding road that led along Lake Travis.

"Where are we going?" she asked. She wasn't in the mood for drinking or dancing or anything else he had in mind. All she wanted was to be back at her place, naked and in bed. A rowdy night of lovemaking was bound to knock her out of the blue mood she'd been fighting all evening.

"I thought a change of scenery would be nice," he said.

His smile was mysterious, his eyes full of repressed laughter. He probably expected her to ask for a better explanation, but she refused to play his game. Crossing her arms over her chest, she stared out the truck window, her bad mood getting worse.

After a while, he turned off onto a side road, then onto a smaller dirt road. He steered the truck over ruts and around holes until they emerged in a wide, grassy spot surrounded by trees and brush. He shut off the engine, and the sudden quiet rang in her ears. He looked at her expectantly.

She reached down and took her phone from her purse. "Is this where I call 911 and tell them you're up to no good out in the middle of nowhere?"

He unsnapped his seat belt and leaned toward her. "I was hoping the two of us might get up to no good together."

His words sent a shiver of excitement through her but she wasn't ready to give up her bad mood just yet. She kept a stern look on her face. "Is this your idea of sexy—making out in your truck in some field?"

He moved closer still and pressed his lips against the soft underside of her neck. "I think anywhere with you is sexy, but who said anything about staying in the truck?"

The words vibrated through her, and the trail of kisses he laid down her throat and across her collarbone set up other vibrations until every nerve hummed with anticipation. "You're crazy," she managed to gasp.

"Absolutely." He unsnapped her seat belt, then reached across and opened the passenger door. "Let's take a little walk," he said.

She got out of the truck and he followed. Taking her

hand, he led her around to the back of the truck. The clearing they were in wasn't very large—maybe twenty yards in diameter, surrounded by tangled knots of scrub oak and yaupon. In the darkness, she could see little beyond the circle of the truck's headlights, but nothing in view struck her as particularly inviting. "You know, I'm not really the outdoorsy type," she said.

"I kind of figured that." He lowered the tailgate of the truck and patted the resulting flat surface. "Sit up here a minute, okay?"

She did as he asked, curiosity overcoming stubbornness. He walked up to the toolbox behind the cab and stripped the cast from his arm. He tossed it into the cab and flexed his fingers.

"How does it feel?" she asked.

"A little tender, but it'll do." He opened the toolbox and pulled out a large plastic trash bag from which he removed several blankets and quilts. Another bag held two pillows, while a third opened to reveal a thick foam pad. Finally he took out a cardboard box and unpacked an oil lamp, which he set on top of the toolbox and lit.

"What are you doing?" she asked, though she was beginning to get the idea.

"No sense being uncomfortable." He unrolled the foam pad into the bed of the truck and topped it with the blankets and pillows. Then he walked around and turned off the headlights. The truck was a dimly lit island now in a sea of darkness.

He walked back around to where she was sitting on the tailgate. "Romantic enough for you?" he asked.

"You're crazy," she said, but she put her arms around his

neck and spread her legs so he could stand between them. He was the perfect height now for kissing, so she did.

She was ready to put her whole body into that kiss, eager to wrap her arms and legs around him, but he held her back, his hands on either side of her rib cage keeping them apart. She gave a low growl of impatience, then forgot everything in the skillful play of lips and tongue. He seemed to find every sensitive nerve in and around her mouth and teased it to full awareness. He nipped and licked and suckled until she was breathless and quivering.

"Who taught you to kiss like that?" she asked when they paused to catch their breaths.

His smile could have melted chocolate. "A gentleman never tells."

"Just as well. If I knew, I'd have to kill her. Right after I thanked her, of course." She brought her lips to his once more, and this time he pulled her close until every possible inch of their bodies touched. The sensitive points of her nipples rubbed against the hard wall of his chest. He slid his hand up her ribs and stroked the sides of her breasts with his thumbs, every touch sending a new shudder of arousal through her.

She wrapped her legs around his hips, the thick ridge of his erection flush against her crotch. She ground against him, both frustrated and excited by the leather and fabric keeping them apart. Instinct drove her to want to get down to the business of satisfying this need within her quickly, but she knew from experience there was even more pleasure to be had in waiting.

He lowered his head and ran his tongue along the top edge of the bustier, then reached up and began unfastening the hooks at the front of the garment, covering each new section of exposed flesh with wet kisses. "Have I mentioned I really like this top?" he said as he worked his way toward her stomach.

"Ah…no. But…thank you." He'd peeled back the satin to expose her breasts and was paying particular attention to her nipples now, which made it difficult to talk. But who needed speech when they were communicating so well without saying a word?

She fumbled with the buttons of his shirt, anxious to feel his skin against her. One button flew off into the darkness and yet another broke in her hand. He laughed and tugged her fingers away. "Better let me or I'll have to buy a new shirt."

"Don't you think clothing is overrated?" she asked with a coy look at her own naked chest.

In a matter of seconds, his shirt joined the button somewhere in the darkness. She hugged him close, pressing her breasts, still wet from his mouth, against the hard heat of his chest. He smoothed his hand down her back, then slipped under the waistband of her pants and cupped her bottom. "It feels so good to have *both* my hands on you," he said.

"This is nice, but there's still too many clothes in the way," she said and reached for his belt buckle.

"I couldn't agree more." In one motion, he pushed the bustier off her shoulders and sent it sailing after his shirt. Then he grasped her waist and bent his head. The next thing she knew, he was lowering the zipper on her pants—with his teeth!

"What are you doing?" She giggled, both aroused and tickled by his "no-hands" approach.

"I'm getting you naked." Except, with his teeth clenched around the zipper, it came out, "I'm gedding oo naketh."

She shook with laughter, but her mirth gave way to moans of pleasure when he stripped off the pants and the silk thong she wore beneath them and pushed her back onto the blankets. The mouth that had proved so dexterous with a zipper proved just as adept at pleasuring her.

Lost in a fog of sensation, she was only faintly aware of him stripping off the rest of his own clothes and joining her on the blankets. His fingers took the place of his mouth on her clit, while his mouth returned to her breasts. She writhed against the onslaught of sensation. The erotic combination of warm night air and Kyle's even warmer mouth and hands made her more aware of her own body than she'd ever been before. Had her breasts always felt so full and aching cradled in a man's palms? Had her stomach ever quivered this way before? she wondered as he traced his tongue around the indentation of her navel. Had her thighs ever trembled like this? she thought as he coaxed them farther apart.

He slid two fingers into her and began to stroke, slow and easy, bringing her to the edge and no further. He raised his head and watched her while his hand continued to work its magic. "Still think this was a bad idea?"

She shook her head. "No." Right now, she couldn't imagine a more wonderful idea. There was something surreal about being here in this nest of blankets and pillows, out in the open but intimately private, alone in the golden halo of lamplight. This was so…romantic. Like something that would happen in a romance novel or the movies. Not to her.

"Look up," he said.

She opened her eyes and stared up at the sky. A thousand pinpricks of light pierced the blackness, and as she watched more appeared, like distant lights twinkling on. And while she was still marveling at the light, Kyle entered her. His face filled her vision and the sensation of him moving in her and over her captured all her senses.

She reached up and grasped his arms, the muscles like sun-warmed iron beneath her fingers. She wanted to hold on to him, to hold on to this moment, but already it was getting away from her. He'd been too skillful at bringing her to the height of arousal, and now she could only surrender and ride desire to the edge and over. If no stars fell, at least a warm, sparkly sensation filled her, as if she'd somehow swallowed starlight.

She kept her eyes closed through the hard thrusts of his own climax, his cries of satisfaction ringing in her ears, the glow of the lantern bright against her eyelids. His hands were strong on her shoulders; his thighs clasping and holding her, not forceful but protective. Any other time she would have balked at the idea, but somehow, for now it felt right.

He lay atop her, his head on her shoulder, his arms keeping most of his weight off her while he remained close. Still connected. She put her arms around him, idly trailing her fingers up and down his spine, feeling the ridge of each vertebra, his skin warm and taut beneath her fingertips. After this night, she thought she might recognize him by touch alone. She remembered the first night they'd been together, when he'd blindfolded her. Had it begun then, her acute awareness of the shape of his muscles, the feel of his skin, the smell of his hair?

"What are you smiling about?" he asked, his voice muffled against her neck.

"How do you know I'm smiling?"

"I can feel your lips curved up where they're pressed against my cheek."

"Maybe you're imagining things."

He raised his head and looked down at her, his grin meeting hers. "So what do you think of my outdoor bedroom?"

"I think it's pretty amazing." She looked up at the stars, unable to stop grinning. This was something she wanted to remember forever. Even when she was old, she'd remember lying here, a goddess in her own secret wilderness.

7

THEY LAY SNUGGLED TOGETHER for a long while, saying nothing. Frankly Kyle didn't think he had the strength to move, but there was something to be said for enjoying the feel of skin on skin. He rested his head against Theresa's breast and breathed in deeply of her perfume—no bottled scent but a mixture of leather and ink and feminine flesh that was uniquely her.

A breeze blew off the lake, sending the lantern flame dancing. Goose pimples puckered on Theresa's arm, and he reached down to pull the quilt up over them.

"How did you know about this place?" she asked.

He slid his hand across her stomach and pulled her closer. "Oh, I came across it a while ago."

"With some other woman?"

He didn't miss the hard edge in her voice. He'd bet she didn't even realize it was there. If he asked her, he was sure she'd say she wasn't the jealous kind. But there it was, that unspoken resentment that he would have brought another woman to this place to do what they had just done together. Come to think of it, he wouldn't have been too keen on the idea of her being out here with some other man.

He opened his eyes and managed to lift his head enough

to look at her. "I have never brought another woman out here," he said. "Not unless you count my sister."

The expression on her face made him wish he had a camera. "What were you doing here with your sister?"

"Oh, you know families. I told her I'd bought some land and she insisted on seeing it."

She shoved up onto her elbows, effectively removing the very comfortable pillow he'd been enjoying. "You own this place?" She glanced around them, but of course it was too dark to see much of anything.

"There's nothing much to see," he said. "It's just vacant land. Five acres of scrub oak and cedar."

"What are you going to do with it?"

"I'm thinking I'll build a house one day." He shrugged. "Of course, that takes regular income. More than I'm bringing in from the rodeo."

She lay back down and allowed him to rest his head on her shoulder again. He could almost feel the curiosity humming through her. Women were like that. They couldn't help it. Good thing, too, he guessed. Men weren't good at talking about details on their own, but it felt good sometimes to have a woman draw things out of you.

He rolled over onto his back and stared up at the stars. His wrist was beginning to ache and he should probably get up and put the cast back on, but he didn't want to move.

Theresa turned onto her side and rested her hand on his chest. It felt good there, connecting them. "What kind of house would you build?" she asked.

"I'm not sure," he said. "I'd like a place with some room, but nothing too big. Lots of wood and tile and glass. If I cut a few trees, I should have a good view of the hills.

Something light and airy—maybe with one of those open floor plans where the rooms sort of flow into each other. And a big deck out back for barbecues and stuff like that."

"High ceilings," she said. "And a big master suite with a big bathtub."

He smiled, picturing her in just such a tub—one big enough for two. "Sounds good," he said. "Now all I need is a job and the money."

"You'll have those one day. You've got the land. That's a good start."

"I guess so." He covered her hand with his own, aware of his heart beating against her palm. "My sister didn't think it was so great. In fact, she said I was a fool to waste my money on something I didn't need."

"Why didn't she think you'd need it?"

"Because she still thinks I'm going to come live on the ranch with her and her husband."

"Oh. But even if you agreed to help run the ranch, what's wrong with having your own place?"

"There are two houses on the ranch. Kristen and her family live in the main house, but I could have the other one. It used to be a bunkhouse, then it was remodeled for a ranch manager to live there. Now it's used as a kind of guesthouse."

"Two houses." She was silent for a long moment, then added, "Do you know I've never lived in a place that wasn't rented? Even the foster families I was with rented houses or apartments."

He heard the longing in her voice and thought of her apartment, so feminine and decorated just so. He guessed even someone as tough and independent as Theresa had a secret longing for a home. Not having that as a kid probably made her want it that much more as an adult. He stroked her hair. "The tattoo shop looks like it's doing pretty well. Couldn't you get a loan and buy a place of your own?"

"Maybe. I guess.... But the shop is really Zach's. I mean, it's half mine, but I never thought of getting a loan on my half. And things are kind of uncertain now, with the protests and everything...."

He frowned. "You don't think this nut, Carter, will succeed in shutting things down, do you?"

"I don't know. I've heard rumors that other businesses are thinking about closing. And times are changing. There are a lot of conservatives in Austin now."

The worry in her voice made him want to find this Carter character and make him eat dirt. "It's not like you're peddling porn movies or selling dope or anything."

"To some people I might as well be." She sighed. "Tattoos and piercings are more accepted now than they've ever been, but they're still not mainstream. And for some people, maintaining the status quo or their idea of 'normal' is more important than anything."

"You know what they say."

"What's that?"

"Normal is just a setting on the dryer."

That surprised a laugh out of her. He smiled and silently congratulated himself on distracting her from her dark mood. No sense brooding over things you couldn't change, after all. Hadn't he told himself that enough times?

They didn't talk for a while after that, content to lie close together and stare up at the stars. His eyes drifted closed, and he was almost asleep when she said, "You could go back to school and learn a new profession, like Zach."

He didn't know whether to be flattered or annoyed that she was so concerned about his future. On the one hand, it was kind of nice to think that someone else gave a damn. On the other, he hadn't asked her to care, had he? "I'm not too keen on the idea of going back to school," he said. "I didn't like it all that much the first go-round. Besides, I'm almost thirty. I've wasted enough time as it is."

"Maybe you could do something related to ranching, but not ranching."

"That was how I got into the rodeo business, remember? What else did you have in mind?"

"I don't know. Horse-trading?"

He laughed and hugged her close. "To be a good horse trader, you have to have the ability to bluff. Considering how much I've lost playing poker, I don't think I'd better risk it."

She was silent for a full minute. He considered drifting off again, but he was awake now, aware of the soft curve of her hip pressed against his side and the warm weight of her breast resting on his arm. Who cared about what he did next year or even next week when the next five minutes held so much promise?

"I could teach you to do tattoos."

He suppressed a sigh. She was as bad as his sister. Was it a particularly female trait to try to solve problems by worrying them to death? He rolled onto his side and arranged his leg over hers. With any luck, he could distract her as much as she was distracting him. "You obviously haven't seen me draw. Even my stick people look like mutants."

Her eyes met his, dark and unreadable in the lantern light, but still they caught and held him. "Then what are you going to do?" she asked.

He rested his forehead against her cheek and closed his eyes. "Darlin', if I had a good answer to that one, believe me, I'd tell you." He'd certainly pondered the question enough lately—more so since that calf had grounded him. Whatever he ended up doing, he wanted it to be something that was his own—not a job handed down to him by his family or one he fell into because it was easy. He wanted something he could spend the rest of his life at without being bored. A tall order. Maybe an impossible one. "There's always dancing with Chippendales."

She punched him. "You'd like that, wouldn't you? A bunch of women screaming for you to take it off."

"There's only one woman I want screaming for me now." He levered himself over her, supporting himself with his elbows on either side of her shoulders while he leaned down to kiss her.

She kissed back, arching her body to his. His response was immediate and strong. The urgency of his need for her again so soon surprised him. That calf might have messed up his life in a lot of ways, but he ought to thank the cantankerous beast for this. It had been a long time since he'd met a woman who could turn him on the way Theresa did.

The way things were going between them, he was starting to wish for a long, slow recovery.

THE PROTESTORS WERE OUT IN full force on Sixth Street the next morning. "What's going on?" Theresa asked as she tried to push past a clot of people in front of Esther's Follies comedy show.

"Mr. Carter's called a press conference," a young man volunteered. He stood on tiptoe, craning his neck to see down the street. "I'm hoping to get on TV."

Great. Everybody wanted to be a celebrity. She squirmed through the crowd and continued toward her shop, but the sidewalks were packed, which made for slow going. At least a third of the people here had to be press; she spotted two news vans illegally parked in loading zones, and rumpled-looking types clutching notebooks or cameras were everywhere she looked. One of them made the mistake of blocking the door of Austin Body Art. "Excuse me, miss," he said. "What do you think of all the commotion here this morning?"

She clutched her keys in one hand and razored him with a cutting look. "I think if you don't get out of my way, I'm going to give you a free piercing—in the middle of your forehead."

He blanched and stepped to one side. "I—I'll just put you down as a disgruntled local businessperson."

"Put down whatever you like, just get the hell out of my way."

She slipped into the shop and slammed the door behind her. She wasn't in any mood to deal with this nonsense today. She'd awakened this morning feeling…unsettled. Last night with Kyle had thrown her off balance. Sure, they'd had a great time, but then there'd been that conversation about what he should do with his future. What did *she* care what he did with his life? It wasn't as if she was his mother or something.

But for some reason, right then, lying next to him, it *had* mattered to her. She didn't know what to make of that.

She told herself to stop worrying about it and went to feed the cats. She was trying to figure out how to take out the trash while avoiding reporters when the door burst open and Scott lunged into the room. "It's a circus out there," he said, shoving the door closed and leaning against it. "Crazy 'Clean' Carter's actually hired a *marching band* to precede his limo down the street."

"I've half a mind to call the cops and file a complaint," she fumed. "I could hardly get into the shop this morning." She glared toward the packed sidewalk visible out the front window. "They can't obstruct traffic that way, and they aren't supposed to be parked in no-parking zones. Nobody with legitimate business down here has a chance of getting through."

"It's only one morning. Who cares?" He settled onto the stool behind the counter and flipped on the computer.

"You ought to care," she said. "If we don't get customers, we don't make any money and you'll be out of a job."

"My life's already shot to hell. I might as well be broke, too."

She suppressed a growl. She was in no mood for any kind of pity party this morning—not to mention that kind of attitude was completely unlike Scott. "What's with you?" she said. "Last time I checked, you were young, single and reasonably good-looking—though incredibly vain about it—not to mention white, male and healthy and therefore privileged. What have you got to bitch about?"

He stared at the computer screen and idly tapped a few

keys. "Why do you think Cherry ignores me? Is it because she's a brain and I'm a jock?"

Yes, we have a winner! She might have known his bad mood had something to do with women. Or one particular woman. She leaned across the counter and prepared to play Mother Confessor. "Maybe she goes for guys who aren't quite so full of themselves."

He swiveled to face her. "Hey, I'm plenty modest." He frowned. "She's the one who's full of herself. She thinks she's so smart. Too smart for me."

He was on to something there. For someone so young, Cherry was almost *too* sure of herself. Theresa felt a twinge of sympathy for Scott. "I wouldn't call you dumb. You set up that whole computer inventory system and our new Web site and everything."

He frowned. "But that's just computers. Kids learn that stuff in kindergarten practically."

She punched him in the arm. "Go ahead and make me feel like Methuselah's grandmother then. *I* didn't learn that stuff. And I'll bet Cherry doesn't know how to do all that, either." Though she wouldn't bet big money. The girl did seem to be awfully smart. Scary smart, really.

"She plays classical music. In a *symphony*." He shook his head. "I mean, come on."

"Good point." She crossed her arms over her chest and studied him critically. As usual, he looked as if he'd just stepped out of an Abercrombie & Fitch catalog: artfully rumpled olive-colored cargo shorts, a tight, faded-just-so T-shirt advertising him as Life Of The Party and dark blue rubber flip-flops, the kind she used to only associate with jail detainees and poor little kids. The whole ensemble probably cost more than half of Cherry's entire haute-hippie wardrobe. "The two of you don't seem to have much at all in common. So why are you even interested in this girl? I mean, from the way you talk, you already have more chicks than you can handle."

He made a face. "Well, yeah. But I was just having fun with those chicks. It didn't mean anything."

"And Cherry means something?" She raised one eyebrow. "Come on, you hardly know her."

He shifted on the stool and looked decidedly uncomfortable. "Sometimes you don't have to know someone very long to just *know*. You know?"

She shook her head.

He twisted his hands together. "It's just…when she's here, I can't stop looking at her and talking to her and wanting her to talk to me. And when she's not here, I can't think about anything else. I mean, I went out last night and I hardly even looked at other women." His expression was bleak. "I've lost interest in anyone else."

"You don't think it's just because she's the first woman—besides me, of course—who hasn't fallen for your dubious charms?"

"No. Because sometimes when we do talk, we get along real well." He leaned toward her, eyes alight. "I think she might even like me. But then I'll say something dumb—or she'll make me think I said something dumb—and she's back to ignoring me. Or playing that damn cello."

"Wait a minute. You're jealous of a *cello?*"

"Have you seen her play that thing? I mean, it's downright sexual—it's between her legs and she's hugging it and leaning her head on it and…"

"You are sick!" She slapped his shoulder. "Get a grip."

His shoulders dropped. "I know. I *feel* sick." His eyes met hers. "Do you think that means I'm really in love?"

She took a step back. "How would I know?"

"Well, you're older and I just figured…"

She shook her head. "You figured wrong." The whole idea was ridiculous.

Some of the life came back into his face. "You're not telling me you've never been in love? Not ever?"

"No. Of course not." She tucked a lock of hair behind one ear. "I mean, once when I was younger I thought…" She shook her head. Even now, that memory made her a little queasy. "But I was wrong. I was just a stupid kid."

"What happened?"

She took another step back. "Oh, no. I'm not spilling my guts to you. You leave my personal life out of this."

"But what am I going to do about Cherry?"

"Nothing. If she likes you, she likes you. But don't try to force the issue." She shook her finger at him. "If I hear one complaint from her about you harassing her, your ass will be out the door. Understand?"

He slumped over the counter, chin in his hands. "I understand."

She retreated to the back room and took a Red Bull from the refrigerator, then put it back and pulled out a Mountain Dew. A morning like this called for serious caffeine and sugar. Between waking to memories of last night with Kyle, doing battle with the protesters, then dealing with Scott's lovesick laments, she'd ridden an emotional roller coaster—and it wasn't even noon.

She sat at the small table in the back room and sucked

down the soda, fighting a wholly uncharacteristic weepiness. Maybe it was PMS, except she'd never had much problem in that area. She knocked firmly on the tabletop.

It was probably all Scott's talk about love. That was enough to make anybody blue. Since foolishly allowing her heart to be stomped flat before she was even old enough to legally buy a drink, she'd assiduously avoided anything to do with the *L* word.

She was mature enough now to concede that all men were not the loathsome, lying scum that the man who'd broken her heart had been. After all, her own brother was a class act. And she'd met a few decent-seeming guys here and there that she could concede might make good relationship material for some women. And Kyle…she'd nominate him as one of the good ones, too.

But that didn't mean that she was trusting herself with any of them. There were too many ways for things to go wrong in the relationship game, and it hurt too much when you tried to put the pieces back together.

Which was why this whole arrangement with Kyle was so ideal. She'd counted on great sex, but he'd given her laughter and romance and the whole nine yards.

Last night—last night had been magic! She'd never forget lying there in the back of his truck, in that nest of blankets, staring up at the stars. A woman could get by a long time on that memory alone.

"Hey, Theresa! Someone here to see you."

She tossed her empty can into the recycling bin and went up front, surprised but pleased at the thought of a customer. Surprise turned to shock when she saw Kyle, his arms full of boxes.

"What's all this?" she asked as she and Scott relieved him of his load.

"I met the UPS man up on the corner. He was trying to fight his way through the crowd to make it here." He set the last box on the end of the counter and grinned at her. "When I saw the crowd, I thought maybe you could use some reinforcements."

She grabbed the phone. "That does it. I'm calling the cops. That definitely has to be 'obstruction of trade' or whatever."

"Sounds illegal to me." He leaned back against the counter, legs stretched out in those tight faded jeans. Every nerve in her body remembered how he felt next to her. Inside her.

She sat down as an operator answered the phone. Only half her mind was on her conversation, though—the other half distracted by a certain sexy cowboy.

"What did they say?" Kyle asked when she hung up.

"They took down my information, but I doubt they'll do anything." She shook her head. "After all, the police are in cahoots with the mayor, who's 'Clean' Carter's big bud. It's a joke, really."

"I did what I could for you," he said.

"What do you mean?"

"When I stopped for gas yesterday afternoon, I noticed the Quickie Mart was having a clearance on those temporary rub-on tattoos. Mostly cartoon characters—you know, SpongeBob and Powerpuff Girls. The guy sold me the whole box for five bucks. I was thinking I'd put them all over me and walk in here one day—as a joke, you know. But when I saw the crowd today, I went back to the truck and got them and handed them out to all the protesters' kids."

"Sweet!" Scott crowed. "All the miniature moralcrats will be inked up good. I hope the press gets some good shots of that."

Kyle looked up at the ceiling, feigning innocence. "I might just have pointed out a particularly photogenic tot to one of the news cameramen. As I recall, she had a Powerpuff Girl in the middle of her forehead and Sponge-Bob up and down both arms."

Theresa stared at him. "I could kiss you."

He quirked his brow at her. "Nothing's stopping you, darlin'."

So she did, aware of Scott, goggle-eyed behind the counter.

"Um, maybe you two should get a room," Scott said after a minute.

"Don't mind him," she said. "He's just in a sour mood because the woman of his dreams won't give him the time of day."

Kyle gave Scott a sympathetic look. "In my experience, the ones who ignore you the most are sometimes the ones who want you in the worst way."

Scott brightened. "Really?"

"That's the thing about women." Kyle directed a look at Theresa. "They can be really contrary."

Ignoring them both, she carried a box over to the workbench and began unpacking it. "I don't know why I ordered so much stuff," she said. "With that bunch out there hounding us, we'll be lucky to get enough customers to pay the rent."

"It's not that bad, is it?" Kyle came to stand behind her.

"We only have two appointments on the book today,"

Scott said. "But Cherry said she might talk a couple of friends from school into checking us out this afternoon."

"Then you ought to have plenty of time to do me," Kyle said.

She raised her eyebrows. "*Do* you?"

"Not again!" Scott said. "I told you—get a room. Or at least wait till I go to lunch."

Kyle sat in the tattoo chair and rolled up his sleeve. "I've decided I want a tattoo."

She set aside the box. "I thought you said you didn't need any decoration."

"You've given me a new appreciation for the art." He grinned. "Besides, I hear they're a big hit with Chippendales' clientele."

"Do you know what you want?"

"I want a stallion."

"A stallion?" She arched one eyebrow. Was this supposed to be a reference to his sexual prowess? "Are you trying to advertise?"

He flushed beneath his tan. "A wild mustang. And it has nothing to do with sex."

She forced herself to look him in the eye, though her mind had definitely wandered farther south. "Okay, so why a wild mustang?"

"They're just about the most independent cusses you'll ever meet."

She laughed. "So you see yourself as having something in common?"

"Let's just say I like to go my own way. Thought it might be good to send the message right here on my arm."

She thought a moment, then took a pen and drew on his

bicep. His arm was hard, brown and sexy as hell, though why this one should be any sexier than the hundreds of others she'd decorated she didn't want to think about too much. "How's that?" She handed him a mirror.

He studied the design of a horse reared up on its hind legs, pawing at the air, and grinned. "You draw a heck of a lot better than I do." He returned the mirror. "I'll take it."

"Are you sure? It's permanent, you know."

"I know." He lay back in the chair. "Do your worst."

She'd finished prepping him and was ready to start the needlework when they heard sirens. Scott went to the front window and looked out. "Uh-oh," he said.

"What is it?"

"Looks like the police chief. And he's headed this way."

8

"THE POLICE CHIEF? Are you sure?" Theresa set aside the tattoo machine and stripped off her latex gloves.

"I've never met the dude, but I've seen his picture in the paper enough. I'm pretty sure that's him."

She joined Scott at the front counter and stared out the window at the tall, broad-shouldered man who was making his way through the crowd toward the shop. "That's him all right." She felt as if she'd swallowed rocks. If Grant Truitt was showing up here, it couldn't be good.

"I'm impressed." Kyle came to stand beside her. "Not only did the cops not ignore your call, they sent the head honcho."

She shook her head. "I don't think that's good news. We've had some run-ins with the chief before."

"Yeah," Scott agreed. "I guess you could say there's bad blood between us."

Of course she hadn't seen him since the day he and Zach had apparently made their peace, but as far as she knew, he still had a poor opinion of Austin Body Art. After all, he'd been one of the chief instigators of the mayor's original Family-Friendly Austin campaign. It stood to reason he was "Clean" Carter's buddy, too.

The door to the shop opened and Chief Truitt stepped inside, followed by a uniformed officer. "I understand someone from here called in a complaint?"

"I did." She stepped forward, hands at her sides, not sure if she should offer to shake or keep her distance. Seeing the frown on his face, she opted for remaining aloof. "The crowd out there is blocking the entrance to my place of business. My customers can't get through." She nodded to the packages still stacked on the counter. "The UPS man couldn't even get past them to make his delivery."

He nodded. "It's Theresa, isn't it?"

"That's right. Theresa Jacobs."

"I'm not likely to forget the last name, am I?" He looked around the shop, his eyes coming to rest on the framed oil painting over the cash register. "That's new, isn't it?"

She followed his gaze to the painting. "Zach sent it last month."

He nodded. "I thought I recognized his work." He glanced at her. "He still hasn't given me one for my collection. I've even offered to pay him, but he won't hear of it."

She suppressed a smile. If she knew her brother, he was enjoying making his former enemy beg for a painting. "He's probably waiting for exactly the right work."

"That's what he tells me." He put his hand on the doorknob. "Sorry about the trouble with the crowd. We'll take care of them."

He nodded to the others, then left, the uniformed officer trailing in his wake. As soon as the door shut, Kyle turned to Theresa. "That didn't sound like bad blood to me. He talked like he and your brother know each other pretty well."

She nodded. "I guess they do, since Zach is seeing his daughter."

"Whoa." Kyle looked toward the chief, who was moving away from them through the crowd, then turned back to Theresa. "Your brother's girlfriend is the police chief's daughter?"

She nodded. "Jen Truitt is a dancer with a hip-hop revue in Chicago."

He grinned. "I get it. So that's why Zach is going to art school in Chicago instead of here. And the chief is apparently an admirer of his art."

"He's a big art collector. He's got a room full of paintings and stuff at his house."

"You've been there?"

She shrugged. "Once." It still felt awkward thinking of herself as being on friendly terms with the most powerful law-enforcement officer in the city. She'd spent too many years avoiding anything to do with the cops.

"Hey, the crowd's moving away from the doors." Scott stood and walked to the window. "There's a whole bunch of cops telling them to get out of the way."

She watched in amazement as the walkway in front of the shop cleared. The crowd gradually retreated all the way to the corner.

She stepped out onto the sidewalk, followed by Kyle and Scott. Chief Truitt was standing across the street, talking with a scowling man in a white shirt and bright red tie.

"Who's that he's talking to?" Kyle asked.

"That's Darryl 'Clean' Carter."

"He doesn't look too happy at the moment."

"No. He looks pretty pissed." In fact, he was gesturing wildly, all red-faced and squinty-eyed. But the chief looked unfazed. He merely shook his head and pointed down the street. After a tense few minutes, Carter stalked away and Truitt headed back toward his car.

Theresa rushed out the door and across the street and intercepted him. "Chief, wait," she called.

He turned and waited for her to catch up. "Is there something else?"

"I just wanted to thank you for getting rid of the crowd."

"I merely pointed out that the right to assemble does not include the right to obstruct the sidewalk or interfere with access to a business. City ordinances require people to remain a reasonable distance from all rights-of-way."

"Mr. Carter didn't look too happy about it."

"I learned early on that if I was doing my job right, there would always be someone unhappy with me."

She couldn't help but smile at that. "But I thought you were on his side."

"I'm on the side of the law. And the law says you have a right to conduct business without being harassed."

"Still, I thought you didn't approve of my business." She straightened. "I seem to recall you making an effort to shut it down not that long ago."

He frowned. "I guess I've changed my mind about a few things since then."

"What? You decided tattoos are a good thing?" She grinned. "Whenever you're ready, I'll do you a tat—on the house."

His frown deepened. "I have no desire to get a tattoo.

But I've accepted that it's the fashion these days. And I certainly know there are far worse things people could be doing—and are doing. Now I'd better get back to work."

"Thanks, anyway. No matter what you say, I know you didn't have to personally come here to take care of this. I appreciate it."

"Make sure your brother knows that. Tell him I'm still waiting for my painting."

"I'll do that." She watched as he got into his car and drove away, then she walked back across the street to Kyle.

"Everything okay?" he asked.

She nodded. "It's better. Come on inside and we'll finish that tattoo."

"All right. Then can we go have lunch somewhere? All this politicking is giving me an appetite."

"When I get through with you, you may have lost your appetite."

The faint lines around his eyes deepened. "What are you talking about? People get tattoos all the time."

"Yes, but it's only fair to warn you—the biggest, toughest guys often end up being the ones who whimper the most."

"You'd like that, wouldn't you—making me whimper?"

She looked him up and down, making sure he registered the heat in her gaze. "Oh, yeah. I'd love to hear you beg me to put you out of your misery."

"Is that a promise?" He leaned close, his hot breath against her ear sending a shiver up her spine. "Because I'd love to see you try."

She chuckled and slicked her tongue across her lips. Maybe they could have more than food for lunch. After all, her apartment wasn't that far away....

"Cut it out, you two," Scott said from his perch behind the counter. "You keep looking at each other like that and I'm going to have to go home and take a cold shower."

She hooked her finger in Kyle's belt loop and tugged him toward the chair. "Come on, hot stuff. Let's get that tattoo. See what you're made of."

Later maybe they'd discuss the whole begging scenario. After all, they had more than a month left to keep each other entertained. There were plenty of things they hadn't tried…yet.

LESS THAN AN HOUR LATER, with a slightly sore arm and a thick bandage around his bicep, Kyle escorted Theresa back out onto the now quiet sidewalk. "Clean" Carter and his marching band had disappeared, along with the press corps and most of the demonstrators. "Take away the cameras and everybody goes home, I guess," he said.

"I wish they'd all go home and stay there." She glanced at the few stragglers still waving their signs on the corner. "This is getting really old. They stop every customer who tries to come into the place, and I'm sure they've turned some away. And now that the election is almost here, I've started getting calls from reporters. It's driving me crazy."

"You're tough. You can take it," he said.

"I'm tough all right." But she didn't sound too happy about it. In fact, she hadn't sounded happy about much of anything all morning, but then he guessed he couldn't blame her. Having to deal with a bunch of self-righteous strangers trying to put you out of business was enough to make anyone sour. "Come on. You'll feel better after you eat." He put his arm around her. At least that was what his mom had always preached. Sometimes it was even true.

They headed to Paradise Café and ordered burgers. They found a table by the window and settled in to eat. "So tell me about your brother and the police chief's daughter," Kyle said. "How did those two ever hook up?"

"She came in to get a tattoo, actually." Theresa swirled a French fry through a pool of ketchup. "It was weird, really. One of those things I thought only happened in books or the movies. The minute those two looked at each other, it was like instant connection." A half smile brought out faint dimples at the corners of her mouth. "Zach kept saying it didn't mean anything, but I knew it did. He was different when she was around. Like something had been missing and he'd suddenly found it." She shook her head and popped the fry into her mouth.

"I've known a few people who experienced that." He pulled the onion off his burger and set it aside. "But for most people I know, it comes on gradual. One day they're friends with someone, then they're a little bit better friends and the next thing you know, they're walking down the aisle. Or at least moving in together."

She picked up her burger, then set it back down again, her expression overly casual. "So…have you been in love before?"

"When I was in third grade I was absolutely sure I was going to marry Kara Stanley."

"And who was Kara Stanley?"

"Only the prettiest, sweetest, smartest girl in all of Cypress Creek Elementary School. She had blond pigtails and wore frilly pink dresses and won the spelling bee every year. All the boys wanted to marry her."

"Figures." She took a huge bite of burger and chewed furiously.

He congratulated himself on having dodged a loaded question, but he'd forgotten how tenacious Theresa could be. "Forget puppy love and school crushes," she said between bites of burger. "Have you ever *really* been in love?"

Why was she doing this? If he said yes, he'd been in love half a dozen times since he was sixteen, she'd think he was a fool. If he said he'd never been in love, she'd suspect he was a freak. "I've *thought* I was in love a few times," he said carefully. "But it never worked out."

"What happened?"

"What do you mean, what happened? Lots of things happened. Sometimes we got tired of each other. Or we ended up heading in different directions. One time I caught the woman I *thought* was the love of my life doing the horizontal mambo with my team roping partner." He took a long drink of Coke. "That was the beginning of my solo calf-roping career. So I guess I can't be too upset. I'm a lot better calf roper than I was a heeler or a header. And she turned into a neurotic witch."

"I guess you came out ahead on that one, though it probably didn't seem like it at the time."

"No, it wasn't any fun at the time." He studied her. She was making patterns in the ketchup with a fry, her mind obviously a million miles away. Was she thinking about a former love of her own? And why did this bother him? "It's your turn," he said. "Have *you* ever been in love?"

"Me?" She laughed. "No, I've managed to avoid that."

Her cheeks flushed, and she wouldn't look him in the eye. That gave him some interesting, even useful information: she was a terrible liar.

"I didn't know it was something you could avoid," he said.

He continued eating, his eyes fixed on her, amused by the game of Truth or Dare they seemed to be caught in. Or rather, he was daring her to tell the truth, and she was trying to figure out how to get out of it.

After a moment, she sighed and pushed her plate away from her. "Maybe I thought I was in love once."

"Oh?"

She shifted in her chair. "I was just a kid. Nineteen. I thought I was pretty hot stuff, working weekends as a waitress in this fancy steak house. He was this good-looking executive type—big smile, expensive suits, flashing lots of money around. He asked me out and we started seeing each other pretty regular." She stirred her Coke with her straw. "I fell pretty hard, believed him when he said I was the best thing that ever happened to him."

Listening to her, watching the pain on her face, he got a bad feeling in the pit of his stomach. He wished he'd never asked the question. But he couldn't stop now. "What happened?"

She looked out the window, her expression grim. "He came into the restaurant one night with a gorgeous blonde. They actually sat at one of my tables, and he ignored me all evening while he fawned over her. And everybody who worked there knew I'd been dating the guy, so they all got to see me humiliated. Turned out she was his wife, and that was his subtle way of letting me know we were through."

He clenched his hands into fists, surprised at the anger that choked him. "What a bastard."

"It was my fault for being so trusting and naive. I mean, it's not like there weren't signs." She took a long drink of soda. "But after that I promised myself I'd be more careful."

So careful she'd apparently never let herself get too close to a man again. "Don't tell me one bad apple made you afraid to try again?" he said.

She frowned at him. "Oh, so if you lose an arm playing with hand grenades, you go out and risk the other one?"

"You didn't lose any body parts that I can see."

"That's what it felt like." She picked a piece of lettuce off her plate and popped it into her mouth. "Besides, it wasn't just him. It was other guys, too. They always wanted me to be something I wasn't. Softer, more feminine."

"You look pretty feminine to me." He let his eyes linger on the swell of cleavage at the neckline of her halter top. The way she dressed didn't leave any doubt that she was one-hundred-percent female. Not that he was complaining....

She shrugged. "Enough for a good-time girl. Not enough for a wife. At least that's the way it seems."

"Now wait a minute...." What kind of guys had she been hanging out with that she believed this load of crap?

"No, it's okay," she said. "I know I'm not like that. I like myself this way. That's all that counts."

I like you this way, too. But he didn't say it. She wasn't in the mood to be flattered or placated. He tried another tack. "You know, there are men out there who appreciate a woman who can take care of herself," he said. "Personally I've never been much for the shrinking-violet type."

"You say that now. But the first time the toilet breaks and your wife fixes it without consulting you, or you eat frozen dinners for five nights in a row because she has more important things to do than cook, you won't think it's so wonderful."

"I guess that would depend on the woman and my feelings for her."

She shook her head. "No, really, it's not even your fault. You grew up on a ranch, right? In a traditional family? Dad worked, mom cooked and kept house and looked after the kids."

"*And* mom worked cattle and hauled hay and did everything my dad did. And my dad managed not to starve every year when Mama went to visit her sister for a week."

"But everybody still had their traditional roles, and things ran smoothly as long as they stuck to them. When you try to put someone like me, who isn't so traditional, into the mix, things get all messed up."

"Maybe tradition is overrated. After all, tradition says I should stay on the ranch and keep doing everything my daddy and my granddaddy did. Instead I'm doing everything I can to avoid that."

"Maybe that's why we get along so well." She checked her watch and pushed her chair back. "I'd better get back to the shop. Just in case some customers do decide to show up."

They split the bill and he followed her out onto the sidewalk, his gaze caught by the sway of her hips in the tight jeans she wore. She could protest all she wanted that she wasn't *traditional* or *feminine*. Those were just words, and who gave a damn what they meant? She'd let somebody else's rules and definitions mess with her head, though he suspected that was just an excuse she'd manufactured to keep from getting hurt again. Nothing like public humiliation to make a person skittish for years to come.

They were almost back to the shop when she stopped on the sidewalk and stared at the red, white and blue For Sale sign in the front window of the Waterloo Tavern. "When did that show up?" she asked.

He shook his head. "I haven't been paying attention."

"It wasn't there yesterday, I'm sure. I'd better find out what's going on." She pulled open the heavy oak door and went inside.

The tavern had the cool, dark atmosphere of all really good bars. Faux Tiffany beer lamps cast an amber glow over the dark wood booths and the pool tables lining one wall. The smell of grilled burgers, spicy chicken wings and beer lingered in the air. Kyle followed Theresa up to the wooden bar that ran the length of the room, the brass foot rail worn smooth from decades of boots propped on it. "Hey, Debby." Theresa nodded to the waitress. "Where's Axel?"

"Hey, Axel! T from next door's here to see you."

A balding old man with a face like a bulldog emerged from the back room. When he saw Theresa, his face split into a grin. "Come here, gorgeous, and make an old man happy," he said, holding his arms wide.

Theresa hugged him, then jerked her head toward the sign in the window. "What's with the For Sale sign?"

"What do you think it is? I'm selling this dump. You want to buy it? In which case, it isn't a dump, it's the best bar in the district."

"But why are you selling? I thought they were going to have to carry you out of here in a pine box."

He shook his head. "I just decided it's time to hang it up. My daughter's after me to move down to Houston to be closer to her and the kids. And I'm getting too old for all the shit that's been going on around here lately."

"You mean the protesters?" Kyle stepped forward and offered his hand. "I'm Kyle Cameron. A friend of Theresa's."

The old man looked him up and down and he grinned again. "You don't look like most of Theresa's friends." His gaze fixed on the silver-and-gold buckle on Kyle's belt. "That thing real?"

He glanced at the buckle. "Yeah. First place, calf roping, Fort Worth Stock Show and Rodeo, 1998."

Axel nodded, then turned back to Theresa. "These right-wing nuts can have the whole place for all I care," he said. "I'm gonna find a little place near my kid and spend all day watching game shows and taking naps in the recliner. You come see me sometime."

"I hate to hear that," she said. "The street won't be the same without you here."

"Ah, it'll never be the same again anyway." He nodded to the sign. "You hear of anybody wants to buy a bar, you send 'em to me." He grinned. "And don't be surprised if I send a few lookers over your way. I figure lettin' 'em know I got a good-lookin' neighbor could be a good selling point."

She laughed and punched his shoulder. "You're a dirty old man, you know that?"

"Just a man, sweetheart. A man who appreciates the finer things in life." He waggled his eyebrows and leered at her chest.

She gave him a hug before she and Kyle left. But the

smile she'd worn inside faded as soon as they were on the sidewalk again. "I can't believe he's selling," she said, shaking her head at the real-estate sign. "Those damn protesters are changing everything."

Change is part of life. But that sounded too sanctimonious to his ears, and besides, she needed cheering up, not preaching to. He needed to make her laugh, make her forget her troubles for a while. He rubbed her shoulder. "I'll come by your place tonight."

She shook her head. "I don't think so. I'm in a lousy mood. I wouldn't be good company."

"I'll put you in a better mood." He smiled. "I've got a surprise."

"What is it?" She looked suspicious.

"If I tell you, it wouldn't be a surprise, would it?" He kissed her cheek. "But you'll like it. I promise." And with any luck, he'd like it, too.

9

THERESA WASN'T REALLY IN the mood to see Kyle that night. By the time she got home, all she wanted was to mope and eat chocolate and watch trash TV. But when she switched on the television, the local news was showing coverage of that morning's press conference on Sixth Street. Darryl "Clean" Carter was pontificating on the need to make Austin synonymous with family-friendly entertainment.

"Gag me." She switched off the TV and checked her watch, annoyed to find it was only a little after seven. Kyle had said he would be by around eight. She should have stayed at the shop longer, but with Cherry and Scott both there and business so slow, there was no need for her to hang around. Besides, watching Scott's lame attempts to impress Cherry and Cherry's just as studied efforts to ignore him was getting on her nerves. Honestly, why didn't the girl admit she was attracted to him, and why didn't he quit trying so hard?

She wandered into the kitchen and stared at the refrigerator. She didn't have to open the door to visualize the contents: one almost-empty jar of peanut butter, two Red Bulls, a half-empty case of Mountain Dew, a lump of old cheese, coffee creamer, leftover Chinese takeout and two bottles of white wine. The wine was tempting, but without food to go with it, she'd end up sloshed in no time.

She turned and picked up the phone intending to order a pizza but found herself punching speed dial for Zach's number. She always felt better after she talked to him.

After four rings, the answering machine picked up. "Hello. We're not home now, but leave a mess—"

"Hold on, I've got it." A familiar female voice interrupted the recorded message. "Sorry about that. I was in the other room. Hello?"

"Jen, hi. I'm sorry. I was trying to call Zach. I must have punched the wrong speed-dial button."

"No, that's okay. You got the right number." She heard the clank of an earring against the phone as Jen switched the receiver to her other ear. "It was silly for both of us to pay rent on expensive places, so we're sharing a place now."

Theresa grinned. "You're living together?"

"Well…yes." She heard the smile in Jen's voice and pictured her probably perched on the edge of the bed twirling her long blond hair around one finger. "This way we get to see each other more and we don't waste time commuting between our apartments."

"Does your dad know yet?"

Jen sighed. "No. He'd only get upset."

The chief would be upset all right. He'd had a hard enough time letting his little girl go off to Chicago with Zach. "He's always worried about you being safe, right?" Theresa said. "Maybe you could point out to him how much safer you are with Zach there instead of being alone at night and stuff."

"Hey, that's a good idea. Thanks. I just have to work up

the nerve to tell him before he and Mom come to visit. Hey, I hate to run, but I've got a rehearsal I have to get to. You want to talk to Zach?"

A few seconds later, her brother got on the line. "Hey, sis, what's up?"

She leaned back against the kitchen counter. "I just thought I'd call and see how you were doing."

"I'm doing great. The school is having this juried art show next month and one of my paintings is going to be in it."

"That's terrific. I mean, it is, isn't it? A juried show— that sounds kind of prestigious."

"It is. The professors picked the best work from each class to be in the show. Not everybody made the cut." She heard the pride in his voice, though Zach was never one to brag.

"That's great. I'm really proud of you." She switched the phone to her other ear. "Hey, speaking of paintings, Chief Truitt was in the shop today and he saw the piece you sent me. He said to tell you you still owe him a painting for his collection."

"What was he doing at the shop?" Zach's voice was wary.

She grinned. "He's thinking of getting a big eagle tattooed across his chest. Maybe with an American flag. But don't tell Jen. It's a surprise for her."

"Cute. Now what was he really doing there?"

"Oh, we had a little trouble with protesters blocking the entrance. He came down and ran them off. I guess I had him all wrong. He was actually real decent about the whole thing."

"He's not so bad once you figure him out. So the protesters are still hanging around?"

"Worse than ever. 'Clean' Carter had a big press conference near the shop this morning and the place was packed. Business is way down. I even came home early today. If it keeps up, I may have to let the new girl go."

"Just hang in there. This will blow over sooner or later."

She shook her head. "I don't know. Some folks are already packing up and calling it quits. Axel has the Waterloo Tavern for sale."

"You lie!"

"I wish I did. He says he's moving to Houston to be near his daughter."

"Then this is just an excuse to do something he wanted to do all along."

"I don't know, Zach. It's pretty depressing down here these days."

"Don't let it get you down. Just hang in there. You know you can take money out of savings to make payroll if you need to."

"I know. But I hate to do that. That's your money for school and your future."

"I'm doing okay. I've even sold a few pieces on the side. And there's a shop here where I can work evenings and weekends when I feel like it. Good people."

"Sounds like you're saving a little on rent these days, too."

"We wanted to be together more. With Jen's rehearsals and the performance schedule and my classes and working, it was wild. This gives us more time with each other."

"I think it's a great idea. I'm happy for you. I really am."

"What about you? Are you seeing anybody?"

She stared at the phone. Did he have some brotherly sixth sense or something? Or maybe he'd talked to Scott.

"I'm going out with this guy I met at the shop. Nothing serious. We're just having fun."

"Who is he? One of the regulars? Not that biker, Joe. He always had a crush on you."

She made a face, thinking of the short, portly blonde who had a cartoon of Porky Pig tattooed on his right arm. Unfortunately the artwork only served to call attention to Joe's marked resemblance to the famous animal. "It's nobody you know. He's a cowboy. A rodeo rider. He broke his wrist and is killing time. I thought we might as well kill it together."

"A cowboy, huh? Well that's different. You take care of yourself, okay?"

"Don't I always?"

"I still worry about you down there and me up here."

The concern in his voice made a knot form in her throat. "I'll be okay," she said. "I'll let you go now. Talk to you soon."

"Sure thing."

She hung up the phone and stared at the receiver, swallowing tears. He'd sounded so good. Really happy. That made her miss him that much more.

So he and Jen were living together? About time. She figured before too much longer they'd make it official. A few more years and she could be an aunt.

She liked the sound of that. Not that she was one to go gaga over babies, but a little niece or nephew would be fun.

The doorbell rang, knocking the warm, fuzzy thoughts right out of her head. She went to answer it and found Kyle tricked out in full western regalia—hat, chaps, leather vest, even boots with spurs.

"The Fat Stock Show isn't until next February," she said.

"This is my surprise." He walked past her and she noticed he was carrying a boom box.

She shut the door and locked it. "What is this?"

"First off, you have to promise not to laugh."

She shook her head. "I don't think I can promise that."

He set down the boom box, then stripped off the cast and dropped it on the floor beside the stereo. He took hold of her arm and steered her to the sofa. "You just sit there and play along, okay? I'm doing this for you."

"Doing what for me? And why do you think I need you to do anything?" But she sat in the center of the sofa, arms folded across her chest.

"I know you've been down about everything that's going on at work and all. I thought this might distract you." He looked around the room. "Now first, we need a little stage setting." He moved a lamp and tilted it to serve as a makeshift spotlight. Then he pulled the coffee table out a little. He started toward the boom box, then stopped and turned back to her. "Oh, I almost forgot this." He pulled a wad of bills from his pocket and handed them to her.

She stared at the money. "What in the world…?"

He grinned. "Just wait and you'll see." He punched Play on the boom box, and music with a punchy beat filled the room. A woman began to sing about wanting a cowboy.

Theresa winced as Kyle climbed up onto the coffee table. "Careful," she said.

"Oh, I'll be fine." He struck a pose, hands on his hips, and grinned down at her.

He looked so pleased with himself, she didn't have the heart to tell him she'd been more concerned about the finish on the table than his personal safety. "You're not going

The Harlequin Reader Service® — Here's how it works:

Accepting your 2 free books and gift places you under no obligation to buy anything. You may keep the books and gift and return the shipping statement marked "cancel." If you do not cancel, about a month later we'll send you 4 additional books and bill you just $3.99 each in the U.S., or $4.47 each in Canada, plus 25¢ shipping & handling per book and applicable taxes if any.* That's the complete price and — compared to cover prices of $4.75 each in the U.S. and $5.75 each in Canada — it's quite a bargain! You may cancel at any time, but if you choose to continue, every month we'll send you 4 more books, which you may either purchase at the discount price or return to us and cancel your subscription.

*Terms and prices subject to change without notice. Sales tax applicable in N.Y. Canadian residents will be charged applicable provincial taxes and GST. Credit or debit balances in a customer's account(s) may be offset by any other outstanding balance owed by or to the customer.

NO POSTAGE
NECESSARY
IF MAILED
IN THE
UNITED STATES

BUSINESS REPLY MAIL
FIRST-CLASS MAIL   PERMIT NO. 717-003   BUFFALO, NY

POSTAGE WILL BE PAID BY ADDRESSEE

HARLEQUIN READER SERVICE
3010 WALDEN AVE
PO BOX 1867
BUFFALO NY 14240-9952

If offer card is missing write to: Harlequin Reader Service, 3010 Walden Ave., P.O. Box 1867, Buffalo NY 14240-1867

GET FREE BOOKS and a FREE GIFT WHEN YOU PLAY THE...

SLOT MACHINE GAME!

Just scratch off the silver box with a coin. Then check below to see the gifts you get!

YES! I have scratched off the silver box. Please send me the 2 free Harlequin Blaze™ books and gift for which I qualify. I understand I am under no obligation to purchase any books, as explained on the back of this card.

350 HDL D7W4   **150 HDL D7XJ**

FIRST NAME

LAST NAME

ADDRESS

APT.#

CITY

STATE/PROV.

ZIP/POSTAL CODE

7	7	7
🍒	🍒	🍒
♣	♣	♣
🔔	🔔	🍒

Worth TWO FREE BOOKS plus a BONUS Mystery Gift!

Worth TWO FREE BOOKS!

Worth ONE FREE BOOK!

TRY AGAIN!

www.eHarlequin.com

(H-B-04/05)

Offer limited to one per household and not valid to current Harlequin Blaze™ subscribers. All orders subject to approval.

© 2000 HARLEQUIN ENTERPRISES LTD. ® and TM are trademarks owned and used by the trademark owner and/or its licensee.

to do what I think you're going to do, are you?" she asked, fighting the urge to giggle.

"Hey, I might be on to a second career here." He swiveled his hips in time to the music.

She couldn't help it now. She collapsed against the cushions, laughing.

He pretended to glare at her, though the laughter in his eyes diluted the fierceness of the gaze. "This isn't easy, you know. Give me some credit. How many men do you know who'd make a fool of themselves this way for a woman?"

His words changed her laughter to a deeper emotion. He really meant that, didn't he? He *wanted* her to be happy, even if it meant doing ridiculous things to make her smile. An invisible hand squeezed her heart and she blinked back tears. "I won't laugh anymore, I promise," she said. The trick would be avoiding bursting into tears.

He swiveled and turned and began to get a rhythm. He really wasn't that bad. A little stiff, maybe, but she had to admit he looked good in that outfit. Very masculine. Virile.

His eyes locked with hers, the laughter gone now, replaced by definite heat. He unfastened the top button of his shirt and she began to feel warm, mesmerized by the section of chest revealed with each undone button. Oh, wow. He might really be on to something here. She sat back and tried to relax, fighting a losing battle against the tension coiling within her.

He slipped off the vest. "Hold this." She scarcely had time to put up her hands before he tossed it to her.

She clutched the vest to her nose and inhaled. It smelled like Kyle—dusty leather and outdoors and an underlying sweetness.

"You're supposed to be watching me."

"Yes, sir." She laid the vest aside and focused her attention on him once more. Continuing to sway in time to the music, he slowly pulled his shirttail out of his pants. She caught a glimpse of his stomach and her insides quivered.

He turned his back to her and lowered the shirt over his shoulders. The sight of those tan, muscular shoulders did something to her. He was so strong, yet he could be so gentle.

He let the shirt drop and turned back around, revealing his naked chest. The woman in the song was moaning about riding her cowboy, and Theresa licked her lips. There were definitely a few things she'd like to do with the man in front of her.

"You like what you see?" he asked.

She nodded. "I have to admit, this is kind of sexy."

"You ain't seen nothing yet, darlin'."

With something less than grace, he pulled off first one boot, then the other, sending them thudding to the carpet. The sight of the muscles in his chest and arms flexing stopped her laughter, though.

He began to sway again, putting his hands behind his head, swiveling his hips, then thrusting his pelvis. It would have been comical in another context, but the heat in his eyes, the intent behind the movement, made every gesture incredibly seductive. "Oh, yeah," she murmured.

He loosened the tie at the side of his chaps, then reached for his belt buckle. "You want this off?" he asked.

She nodded. "Yes."

"Then you need to show me the love, honey. You don't

think those guys up there on stage are taking it all off for their own enjoyment, do you?"

She grinned. "Then come here and I'll show you."

He danced to the edge of the table. She reached up and tucked a dollar bill into the waistband of his jeans, sliding her fingers down as far as she could, feeling his stomach contract, the wiry hairs that formed a V toward his crotch brushing against the back of her hand.

She rose, intending to steal a kiss, but he backed away. "Uh, uh, uh." He wagged a finger at her. "They have rules about touching the help, you know."

"I thought that was only in topless bars."

"Maybe so." He shrugged. "That's the only kind I've been in."

She sat back and folded her arms across her chest. "Keep dancing. You have a lot more to take off."

He unhooked the belt buckle and drew the belt oh-so-slowly from the belt loops. Next he undid the top button of his jeans. She was wet with anticipation as she waited for him to lower the zipper. But instead he trailed his fingers up and down that metallic line. His erection was clearly evident now. "It turns me on having you look at me that way," he said.

"Look at you what way?" She tore her gaze from him, but her eyes were drawn back to him by a pull at least as strong as gravity.

"Like you might just self-combust if I don't make love to you."

She squirmed. "I think you're exaggerating."

"You do?" He lowered the zipper a scant inch. "You look pretty hot to me." Another inch. "You make *me* hot."

She swallowed hard, not saying anything.

"You've got more dollars there." He nodded to the wad of money in her lap. "Aren't you going to use them?"

"But what will they buy me?" She leaned forward and tucked a bill in the opening of the zipper, dragging her nails across his erection.

He hissed in a breath and grasped her wrist. "Remember what I said about touching."

She tried for an innocent look. "It was an accident."

He shoved her back. "Sit down and watch."

She did as he asked, enjoying the sharp edge of desire that had ahold of her. Her eyes tracked his hand as he lowered the zipper the rest of the way. His black briefs bulged in the opening, the head of his penis clearly outlined. She chewed her thumb, stifling a groan.

"Think I should take 'em off the rest of the way?" he asked.

"I don't know. Should you?" She traced the neckline of her halter, her nails scraping across her exposed cleavage. Her nipples were hard pearls pressed against the fabric of the top.

Their eyes met and she had trouble breathing. In that one look, she could read everything he wanted to do to her. Everything he *would* do.

He whirled around, putting his back to her, and lowered the jeans, keeping the briefs and chaps in place.

The sight of his ass framed by the leather straps of the chaps made her squeeze her thighs together against the rush of longing. Her hands itched to squeeze his cheeks, to feel her naked breasts against the hard plane of his back.

He turned to face her again and she choked back a moan.

If the view from the back had been enticing, the scene from the front made her want to shout out a big thank you that she was a woman. "You ought to be on a calendar somewhere," she said.

"Why settle for a picture when you can have the real thing?" In one move, he ripped off the briefs. The seams parted and he tossed the resulting rag over his shoulder. He was naked now, except for the chaps and the hat and the bandanna around his neck. Naked and beautiful and sexy as hell.

He shimmied and his erection quivered, beckoning her. He put his hands behind his head and struck a pose. "What do you think? You think I've got what it takes?"

"I don't know about that, but I'm ready to take what you've got." She stood and slipped another bill beneath the strap of the chaps. This time he didn't try to stop her when she cupped him in her hand, his balls velvet-smooth and hot in her palm. She traced one finger around his asshole, then pressed the skin over his scrotum firmly but not too hard. He groaned and steadied himself with his hands on her shoulders.

"Are you feeling better now?" he asked, a little breathless.

She nodded. "Much better." She leaned closer as she spoke, her mouth almost but not quite touching the head of his penis, her warm breath caressing him.

"I'll bet we can make us both feel even better," he said, arching forward slightly, bumping against her mouth.

She took the hint and encircled him with her tongue. His hands on her shoulders tightened and he rocked farther forward.

He was hot and hard and smelled of herbal soap and sex,

and tasted clean and faintly salty. She took as much of him as she could into her mouth, feeling the head bump against the roof of her mouth and the weight of his torso bear down on her shoulders as he tried to steady himself.

She showed no mercy, stroking and sucking, his arousal feeding her own desire.

After a moment, he pulled away, stumbling back. His eyes were glazed and he was breathing hard. "Slow down," he said.

She smiled. "Did you have something else in mind?"

He gave her a greedy look. "I have a lot in mind." He jumped down off the table and pulled her close. Before she could speak, he covered her mouth with his, his kiss demanding, insatiable.

She twined her hands in his hair and arched against him, reveling in the feel of his skin, anxious to be naked herself.

He slipped his hand into the waistband of her jeans, brushing her pubic hair with his fingers. "So watching me turned you on?" he asked.

"What do you think?" She nibbled his earlobe and smoothed her hands down his back.

He pushed his hand lower. "I think it did. You're wet."

She drew back enough to look him in the eye. "You're a lousy dancer, did you know that?"

"I'm a lousy stripper. There are some dances I do very well." He unsnapped her jeans and lowered the zipper.

"Oh, yeah. What did you call it? The horizontal mambo?"

"That's one of them. I'm not bad at the perpendicular polka, either." He moved his hands to her hips and shoved jeans and underwear together toward the floor. "And then there's my personal favorite—the pokey pokey."

"The pokey pokey?" She laughed, even as he slid two fingers into her, turning the laughter into a moan. "What's that?"

"It's first cousin to the hokey pokey, but you don't use your feet." He began to sing softly. "You put one finger in, you put one finger out. You put one finger in and you shake it all about." He demonstrated, kissing his way down the side of her face as he did so. "It also works with other parts."

"I—I think I like that particular dance, too." She had trouble forming words as his fingers continued to stir amazing sensations in her.

He reached back and unfastened her halter, then let the straps fall to her waist, baring her breasts. While his fingers continued their rhythm, he drew one nipple into his mouth. She clutched his shoulders and arched her back against the sharp desire that lanced through her as his teeth lightly grazed her.

With his free hand, he fondled her other breast. "You are so gorgeous," he murmured. "Sometimes I have dreams about you."

"Wh-what kind of dreams?"

"Wet ones."

She closed her eyes and let her head fall back as he transferred his mouth to her other breast. Any minute now, she was sure her knees would buckle and she'd melt at his feet. Or maybe he'd been right earlier when he'd said she would burst into flames.

The next thing she knew, he was leading her to the bedroom. Standing beside her bed, he started to take off the chaps. She put out a hand to stop him. "No. Leave them on."

He grinned. "You like them?"

She put her hands on his waist and gave him an admiring look. "Let's just say I like the way they frame your, um, assets." She reached up and took off his hat. "You can lose this, though."

He pulled her close in another breath-stealing kiss, then they fell onto the bed. She lay back against the pillows while he knelt beside her and rolled on a condom. The sight of him in those chaps and that bandanna and the memory of him dancing just for her—risking dignity and all—overwhelmed her, and she felt herself getting all emotional again. She squeezed her eyes shut against the tears that threatened, even as a fresh wave of need swelled within her.

He entered her slowly, sinking as far as he could go. She moaned in ecstasy and arched up to bring him closer still. "I don't think I can go slow this time, darlin'," he said.

She shook her head. "Then don't go slow. Go fast."

He withdrew and sank into her again, filling her completely with each thrust, leaving her bereft and aching with each withdrawal. Still it wasn't enough, and she writhed beneath him, reaching for feelings that were just beyond her.

When he brought one hand down between them to fondle her clit, she screamed, "Yes!"

His fingers worked their magic, and she went off like a firecracker, intense and burning, little shattering aftershocks rocketing through her, leaving her breathless. She felt tears slip from beneath her tightly shut eyes and tasted salt, but was confident Kyle never noticed, as his own climax overtook him. He shouted her name and pressed her back into the mattress. She wrapped her legs around him, holding him close.

After a few moments, his thrusts slowed, then stopped, and he lowered himself gently over her. "Was it worth the price of admission?" he mumbled against her throat.

She smiled and combed her fingers through his hair. It was slightly damp, curling up at the ends, tickling the palm of her hand. "I'd pay to see it again."

"That's good. But not right now. Not for a few hours." He pressed his forehead against her shoulder, eyes closed, breaths still coming in hard pants. "Maybe not even tomorrow."

"Mmm." She stroked her hand down his back, enjoying the dragging lethargy of being fully sated. She didn't want to think about tomorrow or even the next hour. She was happy and satisfied now—what else mattered? "I don't have anywhere I have to be," she murmured. "Do you?"

He rolled off her and looked down at her, grinning. "Nowhere but here, darlin'. Nowhere but here."

10

KYLE WOKE UP SOME TIME LATER, aware first of Theresa lying beside him, the skin of her thigh satin-soft against him, her breast an enticing weight on his arm. Then he registered the softness of the bed and the sweet-smelling cotton sheets. Sleeping with a woman definitely had more appeal to the senses than grabbing some shut-eye rolled up in a sleeping bag in his horse trailer, or even crawling into the tangled sheets of the bed at his borrowed apartment. Guys liked to think they were tough and didn't need things like perfumed sheets and feather pillows, but give even the most rugged outdoorsman those things and throw in a warm, willing, curvy woman, and any other sleeping arrangements sucked ditch water.

He turned and pulled her close, his hand around her waist, his head next to hers on the pillow. She opened her eyes and smiled at him. "Hey, there."

"Hey, there, yourself." He kissed her cheek. She smelled like vanilla and face powder. A soft, feminine scent.

She turned toward him a little, and her vision focused on his new tattoo. "Your tat turned out nice," she said.

"The artist does good work." He buried his nose in her neck and planted a kiss on her collarbone. He couldn't have slept long, but the little nap had recharged his batteries and the feel of her naked body against his had him ready for action again.

But she was obviously in the mood to talk. "So stallions are really independent?"

"A wild mustang especially. You've heard the expression 'stubborn as a mule'? Well, a mule ain't got nothing on a wild horse. And they're smart, too."

"How do you know so much about it?"

"A few years back I volunteered to help round up a herd of wild horses that was being moved to a sanctuary in Nevada. We spent a week gathering up maybe three dozen animals. And the stallion was the last to come in. He liked to wear us out, leading us in and out of every draw and canyon within fifty miles, doubling back and circling around. Just when we thought we had him cornered, he'd pop up behind us. After a while, every time he whinnied, it sounded like he was laughing at us."

She rested her head on his shoulder. "Independent, stubborn and smart. I can relate."

He smoothed her hair. "Guess folks like us need to stick together. It's getting harder all the time to be a nonconformist, seems like."

"Nah, there's still room for us. We keep things interesting for everybody else." She idly traced patterns in the hair on his chest. The light, tickling touches were sending definite messages below the belt. He was getting downright anxious for round two. Just to make sure she got the idea, he brought his hand up and began stroking the side of her breast.

She squirmed but didn't stop him. "Speaking of nonconformists, I talked to Zach this afternoon."

"What's he up to?"

"He sounded good. One of his paintings has been chosen for an exhibition. I guess it's kind of a big deal." But she didn't sound particularly thrilled about the news. She sounded sad.

He stopped fondling and hugged her close. "You miss him, don't you?"

She nodded, her chin brushing against his chest. "Yes, but he's so happy now. And I want him to be happy."

He stroked his thumb along her cheek. "What about you? You deserve to be happy, too."

"Yeah. I do."

He smiled at the certainty behind the words. Count on Theresa not to wallow in self-pity. It was one of the things he admired most about her. "So what would make you happy?"

"Does anybody know that? I mean, if there was a book you could look up the answer to that question in, it would make billions."

"What do you *think* would make you happy?"

She shook her head. "I can't tell you."

The answer struck him as odd. He slid out from under her and propped himself up on one elbow so that he could see her face. "Because you don't know or because you don't trust me with the answer?"

She smoothed the sheet between them, her eyes following the movement of her hand. "Maybe I don't trust myself."

He kissed her shoulder. "You're a strong woman. You can trust yourself."

Then she looked into his eyes. "What do you think would make *you* happy?"

How had this conversation gotten so serious, anyway? He hadn't meant for that to happen. They were here to have a good time. To forget about their problems. He lay back and pulled her over on top of him. "Right now, *this* makes me happy. That's all I need to know."

She stared down into his eyes and fit her crotch more firmly against his. "Right now, this makes me happy, too. This morning I was wondering if I even remembered how to be happy, so I guess that's something."

"Yeah, I'd say it's something." He smoothed his hand across her back until it was resting on the curve of her bottom. He wanted her to be happy. Especially when she was with him. Because he sure as hell felt better around her than at any other time lately. "Why don't you come to the ranch with me this weekend?"

She blinked. "What?"

"I mean it. You could stand to get away from the shop and everything going on down there. And I'd like you to see the place."

Deep frown lines formed between her eyes and she worried her lower lip between her teeth. "I don't know about going away for the weekend…."

"Come on. You don't have other plans, do you? You need a break."

"What will your sister think?"

That she'd even care about his sister's opinion touched him; he'd come to think of her as someone who didn't waste time worrying about what others thought of her. He patted her bottom with both hands. "You won't be what she'll expect at first, but once she gets to know you, I know she'll like you. Besides, we'll stay at the guesthouse. You won't even see her that much." He squeezed her buns, feeling himself grow harder. "The ranch isn't that exciting, but I have a feeling we'll find plenty to *entertain* us." He grinned.

A sultry look wiped out the nervousness he thought he'd glimpsed in her eyes. "All right. I'll do it. I'll admit I've always wondered what it would be like to have a *real* roll in the hay."

"From what I remember, it's itchy." He rolled them both onto their sides and lowered his head to kiss the top of her breast.

"Oh, so you take women home to the ranch all the time?" Her tone had an edge beyond teasing.

He smiled, then closed his lips over her nipple, enjoying the way she suddenly arched against him. "Not unless you count Becky Sue Frazier in eleventh grade. And she wasn't there for the weekend, only one afternoon. And she fussed at me for messing up her hair and getting chaff down her underwear." Theresa's nipple was wet and very pink now; a hard, sensitive nub against his tongue. "I don't think she enjoyed the afternoon nearly as much as I did."

"Oh. So you haven't taken a girl home since then?"

"Nope." He'd always made it a point to keep his personal life separate from his family life. Not to mention, he didn't want to give his sister any ideas. He always figured if he brought a gal home, she'd start picking out a dress to wear to the wedding. But he didn't have to worry about that with Theresa. Kristen would take one look at the leather-clad tattoo artist and all thoughts of wedding planning would fly right out of her head.

He transferred his attention to the other nipple. Theresa

was breathing hard now. He loved that she was so responsive. Listening to her get turned on was a huge turn-on for him, too. "I think it's time for another dancing lesson," he said.

"The perpendicular polka?"

"Maybe." He slid down her body, pausing to suckle gently at her navel. "It'll be a surprise."

"I'm beginning to like your surprises."

"That's good, because I'm full of them. Sometimes I even surprise myself."

Inviting her to the ranch had been a surprise; something he hadn't planned. But what the heck, they'd have a good time. He and Theresa always had a good time together. How many people in his life could he say that about?

He slid lower until his mouth hovered over her clit, his hands on her thighs. "Should I keep going?" he asked—a purely rhetorical question, he was sure.

She arched toward him. "What do you think?"

"I think I'll keep going." He lowered his mouth on her and she let out a low moan.

"That's good," she whispered. "Don't stop. Whatever you do, don't stop."

THERESA TOLD HERSELF THERE was no reason for her to feel funny about going away for the weekend with Kyle. After all, people took trips together all the time and it didn't necessarily mean anything. Besides, he was absolutely right when he said she needed to get away. A few days away from all the politics and protesters would help her calm down and give her some perspective. And the ranch would be a kick. The closest she'd ever been to a cow was seeing them grazing along the side of the road.

"I'll need you two to cover for me at the shop this weekend," she told Scott and Cherry the afternoon after Kyle issued his invitation. "I'm going out of town."

"Cool. We can handle it." Scott grinned at Cherry, who quickly looked away.

"So where are you going?" Cherry asked.

"Oh, just on a short trip." Theresa waved her hand, as if the destination was of no consequence.

"You going by yourself?" Scott asked.

"Since when are you so nosy?" she asked.

He grinned. "You must be going with someone if you're getting so bent about a simple question." He looked at Cherry. "I bet it's that cowboy."

"His name is Kyle." Theresa snatched up the schedule book and flipped to the appointments for Saturday. "Now can the two of you figure out who works when, or do I have to sit down and make you a schedule?"

"We'll work it out," Cherry said. "I have a performance Saturday evening, but I can work before and after that as long as I can practice here."

"I don't see any problem with that." Theresa gave Scott a stern look. "Do you, Scott?"

Two patches of red showed high on his cheekbones, but he stuck up his chin and shrugged. "I don't care if she plays. Maybe it'll make those sign carriers think we're highbrow."

"Maybe so," Theresa said. Except the musician had spiky red hair and tattoos. "What about you, Scott? Are you free to work all weekend?"

He shrugged again, a gesture that was really beginning to annoy her. "I know a few chicks will be disappointed, but I'll make it up to them."

"Oh, you are so full of it." Cherry glared at him, then marched toward the back room.

Theresa leaned toward Scott and lowered her voice. "Pouring it on a little thick, aren't you, Casanova?"

"What? You don't believe a dude like me has chicks lining up for dates with him on a Saturday night? Woman, I have got a serious groove on. I can't believe you and that Cherry chick are dissing me."

She shook her head. "Right, Scott. You're obviously irresistible."

He straightened his shirt collar. "Damn straight I am. But hey, don't you worry about this weekend. I'll hold down the fort."

"Right. And maybe you can use some of that amazing sex appeal of yours to pull in a few more paying customers while you're at it." She glanced down at the appointment book. "This is looking pretty pathetic."

The bells on the back of the door jangled and Madeline breezed in. "Hey, girl," she said. "You're looking gorgeous as always." The two friends embraced. "I know you said you weren't interested in joining our campaign, but I thought I'd let you know the plan we've come up with."

"What are you going to do?" Theresa leaned back against the front counter.

"We're mounting a publicity campaign of our own. Our slogan is Save Sixth Street! Austin is known for the music scene and Sixth Street, and we think people need to remember that."

Theresa had to admit the slogan was kind of catchy. "Do you think it will help?"

"It can't hurt can it?" Madeline nodded. "And yes, I

think it will help. We have Save Sixth Street! bumper stick-ers and T-shirts. We're asking all the businesses down here to take some. We're all chipping in to cover the printing costs. The bumper stickers are free to anyone who wants one, and the T-shirts are ten bucks. Who wouldn't pay a ten spot for a cool shirt?"

Theresa grinned. "It sounds great."

"Oh, it gets better. Shannon and the gang at Esther's Fol-lies are writing a skit about 'Clean' Carter's dirty cam-paign, and they're going to make it a part of the show."

Considering that Esther's Follies comedy show was one of the biggest attractions on Sixth Street for both locals and out-of-town visitors, that was good news. "This does sound like a terrific way to fight Carter and his bunch," Theresa said.

"Then will you join us?" Madeline grinned.

Theresa nodded. "Okay. Count me in."

"Great! I knew you'd want to be a part of this."

"But don't ask me to come to a lot of boring meetings."

Madeline laughed. "With our group, the meetings are *anything* but boring. We're having a rally Saturday night. I'll let everyone on the committee know you'll be there."

Theresa's face fell. "I won't be able to make it Satur-day night. I'm going out of town."

Madeline clapped her hands. "A vacation? You?" She laughed. "That's wonderful. Are you going by yourself?"

"Uh, with a friend."

"A *man* friend." Cherry emerged from the back room in time to insert her two cents.

Theresa glared at the girl, but Cherry was too busy watching Scott as he made a show of moving heavy boxes of supplies from one shelf to the other, muscles bulging, to pay any attention to Theresa. She sighed and turned back to Madeline.

The older woman leaned over and punched her on the arm. "You go, girl. Come down to the shop. I have some great new things in." She waggled her eyebrows. "Including some very sexy lingerie."

To her great consternation, Theresa felt her cheeks warm. "I don't think I need anything, really," she said. "This is very casual." Besides, she and Kyle had never bothered with formalities like lingerie before. Though maybe some new silk underwear wouldn't hurt…. "Maybe I'll stop by this afternoon," she said.

"You do that." Madeline moved toward the door. "I have to get back to work now, but I'll tell everyone you're on board. Someone will bring your T-shirts and stickers as soon as they're ready. And if you think of anything else we can do, let me know."

Theresa stared after her friend, absently chewing her lower lip. It was great that the business owners were banding together to fight the protesters, but would it be enough?

"So where are you going this weekend?" Cherry asked. She scooped up one of the cats, Mick, and cuddled him to her chin.

"Oh, uh, Kyle's family's ranch. It's near Wimberley, I think. I guess I should get you the number in case there's an emergency."

"Nah, we've got your cell phone. Besides, nothing's going to happen."

"Nothing I can't handle, anyway," Scott said.

Cherry rolled her eyes in Scott's direction, then looked

back at Theresa. "So he's taking you home to meet the family—that sounds serious."

She shook her head. "No, it's not like that at all. There's nothing serious between me and Kyle." She gripped the countertop until her knuckles ached. "We're just going to get away and have a little fun."

It was all fun and games for the two of them, wasn't it? Neither one of them was interested in settling down. Why spoil a good thing by getting all serious, anyway?

"Nobody ever said falling in love couldn't be fun," Cherry said. "The way I figure, it ought to be."

"Shows what you know then," Theresa mumbled. Cherry was smart about a lot of things but love wasn't one of them, otherwise she'd have picked up on how much Scott was mooning over her and put him out of his misery.

"What was that?" Cherry asked.

"Nothing." She grabbed a magazine from a side table and flipped it open, pretending to concentrate on an article about new tattoo machines. She needed to get her head on straight here. She was obviously getting too emotional about this whole thing with Kyle.

They were friends. Good friends showing each other a good time. She wasn't going to let herself get serious about him or anyone else. Thinking like that was a sure way to end up in trouble.

THE FARTHER SHE GOT FROM Austin, the more uncomfortable Theresa felt. As Kyle's truck sped toward the family ranch Friday morning, she stared at the seeming miles of pastureland stretched out on either side of the road and felt overwhelmed by the sheer *emptiness*. She was used to buildings and people and noise and excitement, not all this *nothing*.

"Relax. Everything is going to be fine," Kyle said.

She straightened and tore her gaze from the side window. "What makes you think I'm nervous?" She crossed her arms, then uncrossed them and smoothed her hands down the thighs of her favorite leather pants.

"You haven't said a word since we turned off 290. Anybody looking at you would think you were on your way to jail instead of a relaxing weekend away." He grinned. "But you don't have anything to worry about. Kristen's a nice person. You'll get along fine."

She tried to coax her face into a more pleasant expression. Okay, so maybe she was a little tense. Only because she hated situations where she didn't know what to expect next. Who didn't? "I'm sure she is a nice person. And no offense, but I'm not worried whether she likes me or not. I accepted a long time ago that I strike certain, well, conventional people the wrong way."

He glanced at her. "Is that why you're dressed to kill today?"

She looked down at her leather pants, high-heeled boots, leather halter top and multiple necklaces and bracelets. She might have dressed in her bad-girl best, but no sense in giving any false impressions. "I like this outfit," she said, glancing in the visor mirror at her heavily mascaraed eyes and red, red lips.

"Oh, I like it, too." He reached over and squeezed her knee. "You look hot. I can't wait to get you alone."

She shifted, ignoring the flare of heat his touch sent through her. Yeah, she'd go for getting him alone. The more time she spent with just him—away from his family—the better she'd feel. Any way you looked at it, she wasn't the kind of woman men brought home for their family's approval. That was another reason for her in-your-face attire. This way, they'd get any doubts out of the way up-front as to exactly what kind of relationship she and Kyle were involved in. A woman dressed the way she was dressed was obviously a passing sexual fling and not a serious girlfriend.

"It's not much farther," he said as they passed a long, low barn and a sign advertising Stud Service. "Maybe another ten, fifteen minutes."

"I can understand why you don't want to live way out here." She gestured to the pastureland around them. "There's nothing and no one out here."

"Believe it or not, it used to be a lot more isolated. Now there are all kinds of people and houses. Some of the old ranches have been sold and the land turned into subdivisions."

"Did your family ever think about doing that?"

He shook his head. "No, and it's probably selfish of me, but I'm glad of it. I may not want to live on the ranch, but part of me likes knowing it's still in the family. Fortunately Kristen and Ken love the place. I can count on them to keep it going."

"Your brother-in-law's name is Ken?" She made a face. "What were your parents' names?"

"Karen and Kurt."

He laughed at her expression. "I know, it's too much, isn't it? Good thing I didn't have any more brothers or sisters or they'd have run out of names that started with *K*."

"What happened to your parents? I mean, if you don't mind my asking."

"I don't mind. My mom died of cancer when I was fifteen. My dad was killed a few years later in an accident. He was coming home from a stock sale one morning. It was raining and the road was slick and he missed a curve. They said he was killed instantly."

"I'm sorry."

"It's okay. Even at the time, torn up as I was, I thought maybe he was happier. He never was the same after Mama died."

"Wow. It's hard to imagine loving someone that much."

He glanced at her. "It is. But I think that's what a really good marriage does for you. You start out thinking you love someone, but after a while you find out you love them even more."

"Like I said, it's hard to imagine." Did marriages like that even exist anymore—if they ever had? Was it possible to live with someone day after day for years and grow closer, instead of further apart? Maybe. She knew a few couples who might qualify, but still, the odds didn't seem to be in anyone's favor to find that kind of, well, *soul mate*. "Who ran the ranch after your father died?" she asked.

"Kristen was twenty-three then. She and Ken had just gotten married and were living on the ranch already. So they took over. I was already on the rodeo circuit. I thought maybe I should quit and come home to help her, but when I visited, it was obvious the two of them were doing a good job and didn't need me."

"But your sister still wants you to live there and help?"

He nodded. "Not because they need the help but because

she's really big on family and everything. She can't understand why I wouldn't *want* to have a part in running the ranch."

"But you've told her how you feel?"

"Hell yes, I've told her. But she only hears what she wants to hear." He shook his head. "She's great, really. I don't want you to get the wrong idea. But when she gets an idea in her head, it's hard to change her mind."

She glanced at the mustang tattoo on his arm. Guess that kind of stubbornness was a family trait.

After a few minutes more, he slowed the truck and turned onto a lane. He shifted into Park and got out to open the gate, then got back in and drove forward. On the other side, he glanced at Theresa. "Ranch etiquette says that the passenger is in charge of opening and closing gates. I'm just telling you that in case you go riding with someone else while you're here this weekend."

"Sure." She unsnapped her seat belt and grasped the door handle. "I can get it."

"You don't have to get it now," he said. "I was just telling you."

"No, I'll do it." She opened the door and slid out of the truck, then hurried back to shut the gate. She had to wrestle with it a little to slide the catch back in the slot, but she finally managed and brushed her hands off on the seat of her pants as she walked back to the truck. One thing she could definitely do was pull her own weight this weekend. She might be a city girl, but that didn't mean she didn't know how to help out.

The curving drive up to the main house was lined with live oaks, their dark, glossy leaves and curving branches forming a shaded alley for the truck to pass through. Kyle stopped outside a chain-link fence that encircled a white-frame house. Two stories high with a broad front porch and rose bushes blooming along the front, the house looked like something out of a storybook. Or a tourist magazine.

The front door burst open, the screen banging against the house, and a petite woman with long brown hair pulled back in a ponytail hurtled out the door and down the crushed-gravel walk. She hesitated only a moment at the gate before throwing it open and rushing into Kyle's arms. "Bubba! I thought you'd never get here!"

The woman was followed at a slower pace by two little blond girls, one of whom carried a diapered baby. They stood on the other side of the fence and stared at Theresa.

"Kris, I want you to meet Theresa."

Theresa gave Kyle's sister credit. She only hesitated half a second, her gaze flickering over her visitor's all-leather outfit and heavy makeup before she plastered a big smile on her face and stuck out her hand. "Theresa, pleased to meet you. Welcome to the Two Ks."

"Pleased to meet you." She brushed her hand across Kristen's, doing her own version of the smile. Hey, if the country girl could fake a welcome, Theresa could do it, too.

"Y'all come on in and have some tea. And I made a cake." Kristen slipped her arms around Kyle's waist. "Lemon pound cake. Your favorite."

"Maybe later. We just stopped by to say hi before we headed over to the guesthouse."

Kristen's smile hardly wavered. "I meant to tell you when you called, but I decided I might as well wait. You can't stay at the guesthouse."

Kyle slipped out of her grasp. "Why not?"

"One of our hands, Rolly Fernandez, is staying there with his family. Their trailer burned in an electrical fire a couple weeks ago and they lost almost everything. So of course we told them they could use the guesthouse as long as they needed. Rolly's a good hand, and we don't want to lose him."

Kyle frowned. "So why didn't you tell me about this on the phone?"

Her smile slipped a little and she glanced at Theresa. "To tell the truth, I was afraid if I did, you'd change your mind about coming to see us. I didn't want to risk it."

Kyle sighed. "You're right about that. Theresa and I just wanted to come up and relax a little."

"And you *can* relax." She patted his shoulder. "Now get your bags out of that truck and I'll show you your rooms." Another tentative look at Theresa. "I'm sure Theresa would like to freshen up a little after that long drive."

"Rooms?" Kyle put the emphasis on the *s*.

She flushed. "Yes, rooms." She glanced toward the gate. "After all, I've got an example to set for the children." She turned to Theresa again, smile back in place. "I put you in the guest room upstairs. It's very nice. It has an antique bed that belonged to our grandparents."

"And where am I staying?" Kyle asked.

Kristen laughed. "In your old room, silly. Kelly said he wouldn't mind sharing at all. Kelly's my oldest boy," she added for Theresa's benefit. "He's out at the corral helping his dad right now. You'll meet him at supper, though."

Kyle collected their bags and they followed Kristen up the walk to the house. He fell into step beside Theresa. "I'm sorry about this," he whispered. "I had no idea."

"It's all right." Maybe it was just as well she and Kyle wouldn't be able to spend too much time alone this weekend. She was going to have a hard enough time keeping her sanity with Rebecca of Sunnybrook Farm and the K Team without dealing with her mixed up feelings for Kyle, too.

11

THERESA HATED BEING CAUGHT off guard like this. She'd told herself she could handle whatever happened this weekend, but things had started off wrong from the start. She'd been expecting Kyle's sister to be hostile. After all, Theresa clearly wasn't the kind of woman Kristen wanted for her brother. And that was fine. If Kristen was snotty, Theresa would be bitchy right back. She'd had a lot of practice snubbing people who snubbed her.

Instead, while Kristen hadn't been overly friendly, she'd been more welcoming than Theresa had expected. She'd ushered Theresa up to the guest room and urged her to make herself right at home. "And if you need anything at all, you just holler," she'd said with a smile that was the feminine version of Kyle's.

Alone now, Theresa sat on the side of the bed and smoothed her hand over the hand-crocheted bedspread. And what a guest room! It was like something out of a dream, full of antiques and lace and flowers; the kind of room Theresa had always wanted, the kind she'd tried to recreate in her apartment. But instead of flea-market finds and thrift-store bargains, this room was filled with family heirlooms.

She leaned forward to examine more closely the crocheted roses on the coverlet. Kristen had said her grandmother had made this. She must have spent hours crocheting such tiny stitches.

A knock on the door made her jump. She smoothed her hands down her thighs and straightened her shoulders. "Come in."

The door creaked open and Kristen's oldest daughter peeked around it. "Hello."

Theresa eyed her warily. "Hello."

The girl came all the way into the room and shut the door behind her. "My name's Kim."

Of course. Another *K* name. "Hi, Kim. I'm Theresa."

The girl nodded solemnly. She looked to be about ten. She had Kyle's chin and his golden-brown eyes and a smattering of freckles across her nose. The two stared at each other for a long moment until Theresa began to feel uncomfortable. "Did you want something?" she asked finally.

"Are you gonna marry Uncle Kyle?"

For a moment, she forgot how to breathe. Her heart fluttered crazily and she stared at the girl. "N-no!" she stammered. "Why would you think that?" Maybe Kristen had sent the girl up here to ferret out information that she was too polite—or too clever—to ask for herself.

Kim shrugged. "He never brought anyone home with him before."

There went that fluttering again. Amazing what nerves would do to a person. She took a deep breath, hoping she looked calmer and more at ease than she felt. "No, I'm not going to marry Kyle. We're friends." She'd intended the word as a G-rated substitute for *lovers,* but it struck her at that moment that the statement was fact. She and Kyle *were* friends. She'd grown to enjoy his company even out of the bedroom. He made her laugh and he was a good listener.

She marveled at the idea. She'd never had a male friend before, unless you counted Zach. And of course, he didn't count because he was her brother. "Where is Kyle now?" she asked.

The girl pushed away from the door and came to stand in front of her. "He and Mama are in the kitchen talking."

She nodded. "Probably about me."

The girl's eyes slid away. "Well, Mama's been real excited about y'all coming to visit. She's spent two days cooking and cleaning." She made a face. "And I had to spend all my time helping." She looked back at Theresa. "I told her you weren't going to notice if the baseboards weren't scrubbed, and it's sure not likely Uncle Kyle cares."

Theresa laughed. "You're right. I don't even notice baseboards. And I've never scrubbed one in my life."

Kim smiled. "Mama said we had to do it to make a good impression. And I think she just wanted to keep busy so the time would go faster."

Was it possible Kristen had been *nervous* about meeting her? "Why was your mother so excited about this visit?" she asked.

The duh look on the girl's face told Theresa she'd just asked a dumb question. "Uncle Kyle is her brother! He's just about our favorite person in the whole world, and Mama's only family besides Daddy and us kids. We have some cousins down near Houston, but Uncle Kyle's the only close relative. And he doesn't visit near enough to suit Mama."

Theresa thought of Zach. He was her only family. They weren't the type to fuss over each other, but when he and Jen came back to visit, she'd probably boss him around, which was just a different kind of fussing, really.

"Whatever they're talking about now, Mama didn't want me to hear," Kim said. "She sent me outside to play."

"But you didn't go outside."

The girl shook her head. "I went out the back and sneaked back in the front. I wanted to talk to you."

Theresa shifted on the bed. "Why?"

Kim took a step closer. "Because you're different." She reached out and brushed her fingers across Theresa's knee. "I never saw anybody with clothes like this except on TV."

Theresa smiled. "I like to dress a little different."

The girl touched the band of flowers encircling Theresa's arm. "You have a lot of tattoos."

"Not so many," Theresa said. "I know people with a lot more."

"Well, you have more than anybody around here." She stared at the tiger. "Did it hurt to get them?"

"Not much." She tugged her vest over so the girl could see the whole tiger. "My brother drew this one for me because he said I was fierce as a tiger."

Kim nodded. "Mama would have a fit if I did something like that."

"It's a big decision. A tattoo is permanent, so it's best done when you're an adult and you're absolutely sure."

"I guess it's not like cutting your hair or something." She fingered her braids. "Mama won't let me do that, either."

"I don't blame your mother. You have very pretty hair." She smiled.

Kim smiled back. "It's not as long as yours."

"I haven't cut mine since I was in sixth grade." One of her foster mothers had insisted on cutting Theresa's hair in a pixie style, saying she didn't have time to take care of long hair. Theresa had cried for a week afterward and vowed to never let anyone cut her hair again.

"I guess long hair's not so bad." She took a step back. "You won't tell anybody I came up here, will you? Mama wouldn't like it."

"I won't tell." She put her hand over her heart. "Promise."

"I'd better go. Mama said you were resting, so I'd better let you rest."

"It was nice meeting you," Theresa said, and she meant it. She didn't usually have much to do with children, but talking with Kim had helped her relax and feel better about this visit.

Of course, it was going to take more than one friendly kid to help her get through this weekend. This wasn't turning out at all like the vacation she'd planned.

"I'M A LITTLE SURPRISED, Kyle. Theresa doesn't seem like your type."

Kyle sat at the kitchen table watching his sister knead bread. Her hair was coming loose from its ponytail and she had a smudge of flour on her nose. To him, she looked more like a kid playing house than a competent ranch manager and the mother of four children. But then again, she apparently still saw him as her little brother. Guess they didn't really know each other as well as they'd thought.

"How would you know what my type is?" he asked.

She punched the lump of dough and folded it over on

itself. "She's certainly not like any other woman you've dated."

"None you've met." He sipped his coffee and enjoyed watching Kristen squirm a little at this reminder that he had a whole life she wasn't a part of. But truly Theresa wasn't like any other woman he'd dated. None of the others had shared her intriguing combination of wild woman and tender girl. And none of the others had sparked the fireworks they'd enjoyed—in bed and out.

"How did you two meet?" Kristen asked.

"At her tattoo shop."

"She owns a tattoo shop?" Kristen's face paled, so that her freckles stood out on her nose.

"Yeah. She's really talented, too." He pushed back his chair and held out his arm to show Kristen his new tat. "She did this one."

"Oh, Kyle." You'd have thought he'd cut off his nose, Kristen sounded so disappointed.

He braced himself for a lecture, but somehow she refrained. He'd give her credit for that, just as he appreciated how she'd welcomed Theresa despite her misgivings.

"So what have you been doing with yourself lately?" she asked, turning her attention once more to the bread. "Besides getting tattooed. Are you working somewhere?"

"Nope." He stretched out his legs in front of him and fought back a wave of guilt. "I'm spending my days playing pool and going to the gym and living off my savings." At least that sounded better than admitting he'd been a lazy bum.

She frowned at him. "Your savings won't last forever. You need to think about your future."

He raised his arm. "I'm rid of this cast in five weeks. I'll still have time to hit a few rodeos, earn some money."

"You can't rodeo forever. And what if the next time you get kicked in the head instead of the arm?" She plopped the lump of dough into a bowl and covered it with a cloth.

"I'm more likely to get hurt working here on the ranch. Didn't you tell me Ken had to have six stitches just a few weeks ago when he ripped open his arm on a piece of barbed wire?"

"Yes, but at least if you were here you'd be working for something you could hold on to into the future." She turned to face him. "I just don't understand why you're so set on turning your back on something that belongs to you. And you're good at ranch work. Ken says you're better with cattle than he'll ever be."

"But I don't like the work." He stood and set his empty coffee mug on the counter beside her. "You just want me here where you can keep an eye on me."

She smiled. "Is that so bad? *Somebody* needs to look after you."

"I do all right looking after myself." He patted her shoulder. "I think I'll go up and see how Theresa is doing."

"All right. We'll have dinner at six."

"Good. That gives me time to take a nap."

"A nap?" She looked alarmed. "You're not coming down with something, are you?"

He stretched his arms over his head. "Nope. But I had to get up before noon to come out here. I'm not used to these early hours."

The tip of her dish towel barely brushed him as he exited the kitchen. Laughing, he climbed the stairs up to the guest room. He'd expected Theresa to join them in the kitchen after "freshening up"—that female code for, what? Going to the bathroom? Redoing her makeup? She'd looked fresh enough to him, but then he'd decided maybe she was just giving him and his sister a chance to be alone. He'd have to make sure she understood that *she* was the one he wanted to be alone with this weekend.

He tapped on her door and when she muttered a greeting he pushed it open. She was seated on the side of the bed. "Hey, there," he said, shutting the door behind him. "How are you doing?"

She looked around the room. "I'm feeling a little like I wandered into the wrong neighborhood." Her gaze met his. "I can't believe I'm the only person in this house whose name doesn't begin with *K*."

"Thank God." He came to stand between her legs and hugged her close. "I might choke on terminal cuteness if I added to the whole *K* thing."

She looked up at him. "What did your sister say about me?"

"That you're different from the other women I've dated."

She frowned. "Is that true?"

"She hasn't met all the women I've dated." He smoothed his hands down her arms. "But it's true."

His hands dropped to her breasts, but she pushed him away. "What's she doing now?"

Why was she so concerned about Kristen? She ought to be concerned about him. "She's in the kitchen cooking the fatted calf for the prodigal."

She made a face. "I should go down and help her. That's what a good guest is supposed to do, right?"

He shook his head. "No. She doesn't like anyone in her kitchen when she's going all out like this." He unbuttoned the top button of her vest and she didn't stop him, which he took as a good sign. With luck, he'd distract her from all thoughts of his sister or this house or anything but the two of them.

"I guess she's excited to have you visiting."

He was more excited about getting Theresa undressed. Ever since they'd stepped into this house, he'd been hot for her. Guess it was the whole idea of getting away with something he wasn't supposed to. But the way she stared at him told him she wasn't going to let him get by without answering the implied question. He shook his head as his fingers continued to work loose her buttons. "I told Kristen not to make a fuss, but I should have saved my breath."

She put her hand over his. "But she has to make a fuss."

"She does?" He stopped fumbling with the button and studied her face. He hadn't pictured Theresa taking his sister's side on any issue. "What makes you say that?"

"You're her only family, really. The way Zach is my only family. So I can see how you're special to her. And she wants you to know that."

He knew that. But discussing his feelings for his sister while trying to seduce his lover was putting a damper on things. He sank down onto the bed beside her and frowned at her. "You don't understand. Kristen always takes this stuff too far. When Zach wanted to go to Chicago, you didn't have a conniption, did you?"

She shook her head. "Of course not."

No, Theresa wasn't the conniption type. That was one of the things he liked about her. "Well, Kristen would. I'm in the same state and she pesters me to come back here. I don't get why Kristen can't let me do what I want with my life."

"I don't know." She smoothed her hands down her thighs, drawing his attention to the way those leather pants clung to her. If he could just get her off the topic of his sister…

"Maybe…maybe it's because I've had a lot of practice giving up stuff, and she hasn't."

Her words hit him in the gut, replacing lust with something even stronger. She looked so calm and unaffected right now, but he could feel the pain behind the words. The fact that she'd even said them—to him—moved him. He put his arm around her. "What do you mean?"

She shrugged. He felt the tension in her shoulders, saw the fine lines tighten around her mouth. "It's just that when I was a kid in foster care, I learned not to get too attached to a room or a toy or a friend—or even a family. Because after a while, I always had to move away to a different family and situation. That's just the way life was."

He pulled her close, an ache around his heart for her. Sure, all she'd been through had made her tough on the outside, but he knew her well enough now to see how soft she really was inside. He wanted to protect that softness, to let her know it was safe to show more of that to him.

She let him hold her, which ratcheted up the tenderness he felt for her another notch. A week ago, he'd have bet she wouldn't have let down her guard this much. Funny how far they'd come in such a short time, how close he felt to her now.

"Kristen hasn't had to give up as many of the things or people she loves," she said. "So maybe that makes it hard for her."

He rested his chin on top of her head and breathed in her sweet scent. Desire was closing in on him again, but something deeper than mere wanting this time. This feeling was more urgent and needy. "I see what you're saying," he said, smoothing his hand over the silken fall of her hair. "But you can't hold another person that way. She needs to understand that."

She looked at him. "Down inside I think she already knows it. She doesn't strike me as dumb."

Looking down at her, he glimpsed the shadowed valley between her breasts and felt a sharp pull of arousal. He didn't just want her now—he had to have her. "I don't want to talk about Kristen anymore." He kissed her, his mouth hard against hers, his hands unfastening the last button and pushing the vest aside, his fingers edging up under her bra to cup her breasts. He could get lost in these kisses, forget everything in the way they made his heart pound and his blood rush. Kissing Theresa was an instant high, better than any drug.

She tried to push him away, her face flushed, her breath coming in pants. "Kyle, what if somebody walks in?"

He heard the real distress in her voice. "I can fix that." He shoved off the bed and three strides took him to the door. He locked it, then moved a chair in front of it for good measure.

She frowned at his efforts. "So they can't get in. They'll still figure out what we're doing in here."

"No they won't." He joined her on the bed once more and took both her hands in his. "The kids are outside playing. Ken's out working and Kristen is up to her elbows in potatoes and pastry." He lay back and pulled her over on top of him. "And I've been horny all day, thinking about getting you alone."

"We're not exactly alone." She glanced back at the door.

Her breath caught as he unhooked her bra and pushed it aside, then sucked her nipple into his mouth. "We're alone in this room." He spoke around her, his voice muffled. "On this bed. Just you and me." He flicked his tongue across the rigid tip, enjoying the feel of her, the sound of her heavy breathing.

"But...but what if...if someone hears us?" She squirmed on top of him, every movement increasing his arousal.

"You'll just have to be quiet." He smiled, remembering how he'd made her scream the last time they'd been together. He transferred his attention to her other breast. "Can you be quiet?" He sucked harder, emphasizing the words.

"I don't know...." Her voice trailed off into a low moan. He shaped his hands to her bottom and pressed her against his erection. He was hard as a rock and he wanted her to feel that—to know she was the one who'd brought him to this.

She tore at his shirt, endangering the buttons. Her nails scratched the sensitive skin of his belly and she planted wet kisses across his chest. "What if I can't keep quiet?" she asked, even as she lowered the zipper of his jeans.

He reached up and jerked the bandanna from around his neck. "You can use this as a gag." He trailed it across her lips, remembering the last time he'd used it in lovemaking—that first night together, when he'd blindfolded her.

Her eyes darkened, and he thought she was remembering that night, too. They'd known each other only one week, and yet so much had passed between them in that short time. They moved in concert now, practiced lovers in tune with one another. Knowing how she looked, how she would respond, what she wanted from him, added to his anticipation and pleasure. And yet he would never fully solve her mystery—a thought that made sex between them all the more exciting.

She rolled away from him and stood to finish undressing. Watching her, he stripped out of his jeans, his erection springing free, hard and aching. She bent to place her boots neatly by the bed and he groaned at the sight of her rounded ass. Standing, he hugged her from behind, his penis nuzzled between her thighs, his chest pressed against her back while he cupped her breasts. "Just so you know, I plan to get you alone as much as possible this weekend," he said, his lips pressed to her neck.

"Is that a promise?" She reached out and folded down the bedspread. Her hand lingered on the lacy coverlet. "This is so pretty," she murmured.

For all her toughness, she always had liked soft, feminine things. She wore leather and denim on the outside, but her underwear was trimmed in lace. And for all her boldness, he'd seen her melt in his arms. He wanted to make her melt again, to burn away every bit of the coldness she used as a defense.

He helped her onto the bed and crawled in beside her to lie facing her, smoothing his hand across her hip and thigh. She had the bandanna wrapped around one hand, a hint of anxiety lingering in her eyes. "It'll be all right," he said, leaning forward to kiss her shoulder.

"When you were a teenager, did you ever sneak girls into your room to have sex?" she asked.

He shook his head. "No." He grinned. "I sneaked into a few girls' rooms, though." He kissed the valley between her breasts, then slid lower, his tongue trailing along her breastbone, lingering in the indentation of her navel, kissing his way to the narrow strip of curls between her thighs. "Don't ask me why, but knowing at any minute the girl's father could burst through the door waving a shotgun made sex even more exciting."

She laughed. "You're a man who likes to live dangerously."

"No, just a man who likes to live...fully." He sucked her clit into his mouth, tasting her arousal, every nerve of his body aware of her response to him. She moaned and clutched at the sheets, writhing beneath him. He spread her thighs wider and teased her without mercy, wanting her to feel everything he could make her feel.

She moaned again, louder, and he felt a thrill of fear. "Use the bandanna," he urged.

She bit down hard on the cloth, the tendons in her neck standing out as she arched to him. Blood pounded at his temples, and even the brush of the sheet against his engorged penis was agony. He slid two fingers into her, groaning softly as she tightened around him, anticipating the moment he would sink into her.

But not yet. He turned his attention again to her clit, stroking and sucking. She was letting go now, losing herself to his touch. He loved watching her abandon herself to pleasure like this, loved knowing she could be that honest with him.

She tensed, every muscle rigid, and then she shook with her release, straining against him, the bandanna gag muffling her cries. Those muffled sounds excited him so that his hands shook as he sheathed himself with a condom.

He focused his gaze on her face as he slid into her. Her eyes were still closed, but she'd never looked more beautiful. He bit his lip to stifle his own cries as she tightened around him. Surely sex had never been this good before. This…complete.

He closed his eyes and thrust hard, giving in to the haze of need that overwhelmed him. He needed this moment. He needed *her.*

The realization both thrilled and scared him. He wasn't a man who needed anyone else, but in a matter of days this woman had captured him completely. And he'd surrendered willingly.

His climax was powerful. Consuming. He rode the waves of desire, thrusting until he was spent, then collapsed and rolled onto his side, holding her close, keeping himself inside her, unwilling to break that connection.

Her arms came around him, clutching him tightly, as if she, too, were reluctant to break the bond between them. He could feel her heart pounding in rhythm with his own, a steady beat that belonged to them alone. Did she feel it, too, this connection between them that went beyond the physical? Was it even possible for two people who'd known each other so short a time to be in this deep?

He stroked her back, trying to breathe around a knot of emotion in his chest. What had he done now? His affair with Theresa was supposed to be all about having fun and filling the empty weeks of his recovery.

He'd never meant to screw it all up by falling in love.

12

THERESA FINALLY PERSUADED Kyle to leave so she could get ready for dinner—not that she had much to do, since she planned on wearing the same clothes she'd arrived in. But she needed some time alone to think and to put on her public face before going downstairs to deal with the K clan.

As she brushed out her hair and applied a fresh coat of mascara and eyeliner, she thought about this afternoon with Kyle. Their lovemaking had been different somehow. More intense. Was it because she was in such unfamiliar surroundings? Or was it the thrill of the forbidden and the risk of being discovered?

She shook her head and reached for a tube of lipstick. Neither of those answers felt right. Lying in Kyle's arms a few moments ago, she'd felt…content. As if everything in her life had suddenly fallen into place perfectly.

But why should she feel that way now—and *here,* of all places? The idea was even more unsettling than Kristen being so nice to her.

She set aside the lipstick, took one last look at herself in the mirror and went downstairs. She heard laughter and the hum of conversation, and followed the sounds to the dining room. Decorated with Laura Ashley wallpaper and golden oak furniture, it looked like a room in a Victorian dollhouse. The kind of dollhouse Theresa had always coveted as a child.

All conversation ceased as she entered the room. At any other time, she'd have tossed off some comment about making a dramatic entrance, but right now she felt like a bug under a microscope. Though she fought not to let her nervousness show on her face, she was relieved when Kyle stepped forward and took her hand. "Come on and meet everybody," he said, his smile reassuring.

He led her first to a short, stocky man with curly brown hair and a perfectly waxed mustache that curled up on each end. "This is Ken, Kristen's better half. Ken, this is Theresa."

Ken grinned and shook her hand, his brown eyes bright with suppressed laughter. "Pleased to meet you. Kristen's always wondering why Kyle won't give the local girls the time of day, and now I know why. They don't grow 'em like you in the country."

His droll expression combined with the impossible mustache made her smile. "I'm definitely a city girl," she said. "But I hope you won't hold that against me."

"Darlin', I wouldn't hold nothing against you. At least not while Kyle here's around to take offense."

"Don't mind him," Kyle slipped his arm around her. "Ken's been married so long, he's just a little jealous."

"Why should he be jealous when he's got me?" Kristen joined them, smiling at her husband.

Ken hugged his wife around the waist. "Kyle ought to be jealous that I found the woman for me a long time ago, while he's been wasting all these years playing the field."

"I promise you I don't consider any of them wasted." Kyle winked at Theresa. Her heart fluttered at the innocent gesture. *Get a grip,* she told herself.

"This is Kelly." Kyle faked a punch at the boy's shoulder. "When I want to upset Kristen, I threaten to teach him all my wicked ways."

The boy's face was tinted crimson as he looked everywhere but directly at Theresa. "Uh, hello. Ma'am."

She managed not to wince at the polite address. In her world, *ma'am* was reserved for grannies. But here things were probably different, so she swallowed the tart comment that rose to her lips and smiled at the boy.

"Come here and meet my absolute best girlfriends." Kyle tugged her toward the sideboard, where Kim and her sister were counting out silverware. "The little one is Karly—with a *K.* And this doll—" he put his hand on the older girl's head "—this is Kim."

"Hi, Kim." Theresa exchanged a secret smile with the girl.

"Their little brother, Kevin, is around here somewhere," Kyle said.

"Mama already fed him and put him down for a nap." Kim made a face. "Otherwise he just makes a big mess at the table."

Kristen summoned them all to the table then, seating Theresa next to Kyle, with Kim, Karly and Kelly across from them. Ken said grace and then began passing platters of chicken-fried steak, sliced tomatoes, mashed potatoes, fresh corn and slices of hot, homemade bread. "Everything looks delicious," Theresa said. If this was a preview of the rest of her meals here, she'd have to be careful or she wouldn't be able to button her jeans by Monday.

"Kyle tells me you own a tattoo parlor," Kristen said as she buttered a slice of bread for Karly.

"My brother and I own it together, yes."

"Oh, wow!" Kelly stared at her bug-eyed, though he jerked his gaze to his plate when she smiled at him.

"That's a rather unusual occupation for a woman, isn't it?" Kristen asked.

"Not really." She stirred gravy into her potatoes. "A lot of women get tattoos these days, and a lot of times they're more comfortable with a woman doing the work. And some guys think women have a lighter touch with the needles, so they prefer it, too."

"Just the thought of needles gives me the willies," Ken volunteered. "But I can see how having a pretty woman to admire while you were getting it done would make things a little easier."

"I should have warned you my husband is an impossible flirt," Kristen said. "Trust me, he's harmless."

Theresa laughed. If anything, Ken's teasing had made her feel more at ease. Maybe this weekend wouldn't be so awkward after all.

"That's me," Ken grinned. "Even the bulls knew I was no real threat, which is why my rodeo career was so short."

"You were a bull rider?" she asked.

"I wouldn't say he ever rode them," Kyle said. "But he was pretty good at getting bucked off."

"Speaking of bulls," Kristen said when the laughter had subsided. "Did Ken tell you we're thinking of selling Old Gold?"

"No kidding?" Kyle cut into his steak. "Thinking it's time to add some new blood to the line?"

"Something like that," Ken said.

"What do you think, Kyle?" Kristen asked. "Should we go for another full-blood Angus, or add one of the new crosses?"

He shrugged. "That's up to y'all. I don't really have a say in it."

"But you do!" The sharpness in Kristen's voice startled everyone. She smoothed her napkin in her lap, regaining her composure. When she looked up again, she was smiling, but Theresa noticed the strain around her eyes. "The Two Ks is still half yours. Of course you have a say in how it's run."

"You and Ken are the ones running the place now. Those decisions are up to you."

Ken started to say something, but a look from Kristen silenced him. "I know you've been away with the rodeo and you haven't had time to get involved with running things, but that's changed now," she said. "This injury is the perfect opportunity for you to get back up to speed on things."

Theresa wondered if the others heard the sigh that escaped Kyle. He laid aside his fork and looked at his sister. "I'm not interested," he said. "You do what you think is right."

Kristen's smile faltered. She leaned toward him, her voice pleading. "I know you say that. And I could understand a young, single man not wanting to be bothered. But that's changing. You're older now. You can't compete in the rodeo forever. Your injury proves that." She glanced at Theresa. "When you settle down and have a family of your own, you'll want a home for them. That home is here. You know that."

Kyle frowned. "I don't want to talk about that now." He picked up his fork again. "Let's just have a nice dinner." He turned to Ken. "Are these tomatoes out of your garden?"

Ken seemed to welcome the change of subject, too. "We've had a bumper crop this year. Funny thing about tomatoes. Some years you don't get any, and the next year you have more than you know what to do with."

As the conversation rambled from gardening to rodeo gossip, Theresa rearranged the food on her plate, her appetite vanished. Why didn't Kyle tell his sister once and for all he was never coming back to the ranch and that was it? He wanted other things in his life—and what was so wrong with that?

Then again, maybe he hadn't told her because he wasn't sure. After all, if all those generations of Camerons had ranched this land, was Kyle really enough of a rebel to turn his back on all that? He was at an age where a lot of men thought about settling down—and you couldn't get much more settled than Laura Ashley wallpaper and Grandmother's crocheted bedspread.

The meal ended with lemon pound cake. "It's Kyle's favorite," Kristen said as she served up thick slices of cake. "Grandmother Cameron's recipe."

Of course. Someone like Kristen probably never used boxed cake mix, much less bought dessert already prepared at the grocery store bakery. "It's delicious," she said somewhat weakly.

"Before you leave, I'll give you the recipe."

Did Kristen really think Theresa was going to be baking cakes for Kyle? "Um, that's okay," she said. "I've never baked a cake in my life."

"You haven't?" Theresa had to hand it to Suzie Home-maker here—she covered her shock pretty well. Her smile brightened a few watts and she brushed crumbs from the tablecloth. "I'll give you the recipe anyway. It's really easy. And it's Kyle's favorite."

"Then maybe you should give the recipe to Uncle Kyle."

Theresa could have kissed Kim. She bit back a smile as Kristen stared at her daughter. "Well, um, yes, I suppose I could," she said.

"Don't bother with the recipe," Kyle said, extending his plate. "But I wouldn't mind another slice of cake."

When they'd finished eating, Kristen started gathering up the dirty dishes. "Let me help you," Theresa said, stacking plates.

"Oh, no! You're our guest." Kristen took the plates from her. "The girls will help me. You go with Kyle and Ken and visit."

The men had already wandered into the living room. As Theresa went in search of them, she checked the hall clock. Barely seven o'clock and already she was bored out of her skull. If she was back home, she'd be working or at least having a good time with friends in one of the Sixth Street bars. Or she and Kyle might be somewhere alone....

Now there was a thought. She felt better. She'd find Kyle and suggest they sneak off.

She found him and Ken in the living room, seated at a wooden card table. "Hey, there she is!" Ken looked up from the box of dominoes he'd just opened. "You're just in time to learn to play Moon."

"Moon?" She glanced at Kyle.

He pulled out the chair next to him and patted it. "Ken's got his heart set on teaching you to play dominoes."

Theresa could not believe she was sitting here listening to a cowboy with a preposterous mustache explain the intricacies of a domino game. Zach would laugh his ass off if he could see her, but then, what could she do?

"Now, Moon is really easy," Ken said as he spread the dominoes on the table. "It's kind of like cards in that you try to match up pairs. First we take out all the blanks except the double blank."

He did this, dumping those tiles back into the box. Then he began turning over the rest of the dominoes and mixing them up. "Each of us will choose seven dominoes and bid how many tricks we think we can catch."

"You didn't know when you came here you'd be turning tricks, did you?" Kyle said.

"*Catching* tricks, not turning them," Ken said. "Now draw your tiles."

They drew and Theresa studied her hand, aware of Kyle watching her. Looking up and finding his whiskey-warm eyes on her made her think of at least a dozen more private games she'd like to play with him.

"You have to bid at least four tricks but not more than seven," Ken instructed. "You get a point for every trick you catch, and if you get set, you lose as many points as you bid. If you go negative, you get a hickey."

Theresa stared at him. "Could you explain that again in English?"

"I understood the hickey part." Kyle waggled his eyebrows at her.

She smiled. You had to admire a guy who could make

even dominoes—a game she associated with groups of old men who chewed tobacco and spat in the dirt—entertaining.

"Let's just play a hand," Ken said. "You'll get the hang of it."

The game proved to be simple after all and more fun than she'd imagined. Soon she was slapping down dominoes and shouting in triumph when she made a bid or howling when Kyle stole her trick. But the fun was spoiled when Kristen joined them. Not that she meant to put a damper on things, but with his wife present, Ken toned down the flirting. And every time Theresa looked up, Kristen was watching Kyle, hurt evident in her eyes.

"I remember when we learned this game," Kristen said as she watched the others play. "From that old ranch hand. What was his name?"

"Ollie Paget," Kyle said. "He had one finger missing from where he'd got it caught in a dally rope."

"And he dipped Red Rose snuff." Kristen laughed. "We played for pennies, and when Mama found out we'd been gambling away our allowance, she had a fit."

"She'd never have known about it if you hadn't squealed," Kyle said.

Kristen made a face. "I thought that would get me my allowance back."

"Instead all it got you was grounded for two weeks."

The domino game abandoned, they fell into reminiscing about childhood pranks. Ken, who'd grown up nearby, joined in. Listening to their tales of roping calves, falling out of trees and riding horses, Theresa felt as if she'd been raised in a foreign country. Seeing how many free games she could rack up at the video arcade and sitting through fourteen showings of *Star Wars* didn't sound very adventurous in comparison to camping out overnight in a tree fort or jumping off cliffs into the creek.

She pushed back her chair and mustered a weary smile. "I can't believe it, but I'm getting sleepy," she said. "I think I'll go on upstairs."

"But it's only eight-thirty," Kristen protested. "I was going to suggest we play Monopoly."

Kyle groaned. "No way am I going to spend a Friday night playing Monopoly with my sister. My rep would be ruined if anyone ever found out."

"You're just saying that because I always win," she said. "I've told you the secret is to buy as many hotels as you can, but you never listen."

"You are way too bossy, did you know that?"

They were still bickering as Theresa climbed the stairs to the guest room. The truth was, weariness dragged at her, but it wasn't a physical tiredness. She was worn out from trying to cope with all the crazy emotions kicking up a fuss inside of her. One minute she was annoyed at Kyle for letting his sister boss him around, another she was asking herself why she cared so much what he did with his life. That led to trying to ignore the crazy way her heart squeezed tight whenever she thought of the day when she and Kyle wouldn't be together anymore. After all, they'd agreed they were only in this for fun.

And they'd certainly had a lot of good times. She couldn't remember enjoying herself more. But when had all this seriousness crept in? All of a sudden, when she thought about Kyle leaving her, she felt as if she might cry.

And she never cried.

Maybe I'm coming down with something, she thought as she stepped into the bathroom and turned on the shower. That was the only logical explanation. After all, it wasn't likely a city girl like her would fall for a cowboy like Kyle, no matter how good he was in bed or how much he made her laugh. Just because there was a lot more to him than she'd thought at first glance didn't mean he was special or anything.

Did it?

SCOTT TALKED CHERRY INTO going to the Save Sixth Street rally with him, which was some progress, he guessed. Except that she spent the whole time paying attention to the speakers and stuff and never once looked at him. He checked his look in a storefront as they walked back to the shop after the rally ended. Maybe he should have worn a different shirt. He had on a cool, retro tie-dye, one that would probably appeal to her granola-girl side.

"Uh-oh." She stopped on the sidewalk, so that he ran into her.

Not that he minded much, he thought as he steadied himself against her. Underneath all those flowing skirts, she had a really nice figure. "What is it?" he asked.

She pointed ahead of them. "I'm pretty sure that's a reporter waiting outside the shop."

He noticed the woman now, a tall, tanned blonde who looked vaguely familiar. "Isn't that Marci what's-her-name from *Nine News*?"

Cherry looked back over her shoulder at him, one eyebrow raised. "You actually watch the news?"

Now that was a low blow. "I'm not camped out in front

of the TV every evening at six, but I'm not a moron, either, you know."

She had the good grace to wince. "Sorry," she muttered.

An apology from Miss Perfect? Maybe there was hope after all. He nudged her forward. "Let's go see what she wants."

"Hi, I'm Marci Andrews from *Nine News*." She greeted them with a wide smile and a surprisingly powerful handshake as Scott unlocked the door. "I'm doing a story on the Save Sixth Street rally and wanted to talk to some of the local businesspeople. Could I have a few minutes of your time?"

"We're not really—"

Scott pushed Cherry into the shop. "I'd be happy to talk to you." He smiled and looked into her eyes. Maybe he'd struck out with Cherry, but this Marci woman was hot. And maybe seeing him flirting with another woman would wake Cherry up to what she was missing.

"Great." Marci entered the shop, followed by an older man with a handheld camera.

"My name's Scott, by the way. Scott Simpson." He offered his hand. When she took it, he kept hold of hers just a little longer than necessary, continuing to look deep into her eyes. Chicks loved a guy who really paid attention to them—or at least seemed to.

"Uh, nice to meet you, Scott." Marci pulled her hand away and turned to Cherry. "How long have you worked here?" she asked.

"Not long." Cherry moved behind the counter. "I'm only here part-time."

"I've been working here four years," Scott said. He struck

a casual pose against the counter, making sure his profile was to the camera. Might as well show off his best side....

"What impact would you say Darryl Carter's Clean Up Austin Campaign has had on businesses in the area?" Marci asked.

"He's scared some people away, but he doesn't have as much influence as he'd like to think. I mean, look at this place. Does it look like a den of iniquity to you?" He swept his hand around the room. Unfortunately he ended up pointing to a particularly wicked-looking flash of a skull with snakes crawling out of it that he'd drawn for a biker. Not exactly hearts and flowers. He moved over to block the flash, but not before he was sure it was immortalized on camera.

"But if Carter hasn't had an impact, why did the business owners feel the need to start their own campaign?" Marci asked.

"That's a good question, Marci." Isn't that what politicians always said when they didn't know the answer? "I think with Carter putting us in the news, we decided to take advantage of the spotlight and let people know all the good things going on here."

Cherry was giving him a strange look, but he ignored her, on a roll. Not only was he good-looking, he had a gift for rhetoric. Maybe *he* should consider a career in politics.

"So you're active in the business owners' coalition?" Marci asked.

Somehow he kept his smile in place while his mind scrambled for an answer. "I wholeheartedly support their efforts," he said. "They're doing really important work." Was he good or what?

"Thank you." Marci nodded to the cameraman. "I think that wraps it up here, Nick. Let's see if we can get sound bites from any of the Esther's Follies troupe."

"Wait, wouldn't you like to stay longer?" Scott intercepted her at the door. "Maybe we could meet for a drink later?"

She shook her head. "I don't think so." She stepped past him and shut the door behind her. He had to jump back to avoid having his nose crushed.

He heard a sound behind him and turned to find Cherry stifling laughter. "What's so funny?" he demanded.

"You! Did you really think that reporter was going to go out with you?"

"Why not?" He struggled for a cool look to cover up his bruised feelings. "She doesn't know what she's missing." He glanced at his reflection in the front window and smoothed back his hair. Was he losing his touch?

"Could you just dump the player attitude?" Cherry asked.

"What attitude?" He turned to face her. "This is me." He was Scott Simpson, ladies' man.

Cherry rolled her eyes. "All you are is attitude. No substance."

Okay, she was starting to annoy him. "That's rich coming from you."

"What do you mean?"

He joined her behind the counter, effectively blocking her escape. "You have a major attitude. You think you're better than everyone else."

Her eyes widened. "That's not true!"

"It is true. You walked in here the first day with a chip on your shoulder. Theresa couldn't even tell you anything because you already knew it all."

She blushed pink. "That's not true. I mean, I wasn't trying to be a smart-ass."

"Well, you were." She deserved to be set straight about her attitude after making those comments about his own 'tude.

"Only because I really wanted the job." She hunched her shoulders. "And maybe—sometimes—I'm a little short with people, but that's only because I get nervous."

"What do you have to be nervous about? You're cute and smart and talented and everything."

She stared at him, clearly stunned. "You really think so?"

He shrugged. "Sure." He figured she already knew that. It was obvious.

She folded her arms across her chest and gave him a long look. "I could say the same thing about you, you know."

He didn't much care for the way she was staring at him—as if he was a specimen under a microscope. "I don't know what you're talking about."

She leaned toward him. "I think I'm getting it now. This whole Don Juan routine of yours is just a front."

"A front? You don't think I'm a hit with women? You come out with me some Saturday night and I'll show you."

She waved his words away as if she was swatting at a pesky fly. "Sure, you're a big flirt and a lot of women like that kind of thing. And you lucked out in the looks department—you and a million other people. Big deal."

Did that mean she thought he was good-looking? Why didn't she just say so then? "Is there a point to this conversation?" he asked.

"The point is, underneath all that macho crap, you're as insecure as anybody else." She poked him in the chest with her finger. "I just realized that."

She thought he was insecure? Maybe a little, if getting tongue-tied around her was insecurity. And striking out with Marci just now had been an ego blow. "I guess all you chicks expect a guy to be perfect, huh? Sorry to disappoint you."

He turned away, then felt her hand on his shoulder. "Hey, I didn't mean to hurt your feelings," she said.

He shrugged her off. "Like I care what you think, anyway." But it surprised him how much it *did* hurt knowing she saw him as flawed.

"No, wait. I said that wrong." She pounded her fist on the countertop, making him jump. "Dammit, I always screw things up."

He turned and their eyes met—hers big and brown and shiny with tears. "Aw, don't cry." Did she know he couldn't take a woman's tears? He was a big wuss that way. He rushed over to her, reaching for her but too afraid to touch her.

She sniffed. "What I meant to say is that I'm *glad* to see you're not perfect."

"You are?"

"Perfect people are real bores, you know?"

"Yeah. I guess they are." He'd never thought of it before, but maybe there was something to be said for flaws. Like the fact that she'd admitted new people and situations made her nervous. It made her more approachable. He nudged her arm. "So maybe we have something in common after all."

She hesitated, then nodded. "Maybe we do."

"So…" He went for broke and took her hand in his. She didn't jerk away from him, so he figured that was a good sign. "So from now on, you won't think you have to know everything."

"And you'll stop trying to impress me with what a ladies' man you are." She smiled, and her eyes lost their sadness. "Because really, I was already impressed."

If hearts did backflips, his executed a triple somersault. "You were?"

She nodded. "Yeah. You're a really nice guy when you're not trying so hard."

"And you're a really nice girl when you relax a little." He bent to kiss her but froze halfway, still afraid she was going to turn on him.

He didn't have to worry, though. She slipped her free hand around his neck and pulled him down to her. She might not know everything, but she proved she knew how to kiss.

He didn't even hear the bells on the door ring. When she pulled away, she looked as dazed as he felt. "We have a customer," she whispered.

"We do?" He grinned at her, a stupid grin, he was sure, but he couldn't make his mouth move any other way.

She nodded and pointed behind them. "We'd better get to work."

"Right." Work. He was sure he was never going to look at his job—or his co-worker—in the same way again. In fact, if anyone had asked, he would have said everything was just…perfect.

THERESA WOKE TO THE SMELL of brewing coffee and frying bacon and bright sunlight streaming through the window. Shielding her eyes against the glare, she groaned and squinted at the clock. Six-thirty in the morning. She fell back on the pillow and shut her eyes tight, but the bright light seeped through her eyelids, driving out all chances of returning to sleep.

She could hear the others bustling about below—muttered voices, the scrape of silverware against pots and pans. They were probably thinking evil thoughts about lazy city folks who lolled around in bed all day.

Muttering curses, she threw the covers aside and sat up. Not that she cared what the K clan thought of her, but her stomach was growling. Coffee and bacon and whatever else went with it sounded awfully good.

She found Kyle nursing a cup of coffee at the kitchen table. He managed a grunt in greeting, and she smiled in satisfaction. He didn't look any more awake than she felt.

"Good morning, Theresa." Kristen looked up from a bowl of eggs she was beating into submission and spoke far too cheerfully for this time of day.

"Morning," Theresa managed and made a beeline for the coffeepot.

"I hope I didn't wake you," Kristen said, continuing to whip the eggs. "Kyle said he didn't think you normally got up this early."

"He's right." She glanced at the man slumped at the table. "I don't think Kyle gets up this early, either."

"I know, but the girls wanted to see their uncle before they left for 4-H camp." She poured the eggs into a big iron skillet, where they sizzled and bubbled violently. "I knew it wouldn't kill him to get up and say hello."

"It might." He set his empty mug on the table with a thud. "No sane person should be up at this hour."

"Don't be silly. This is my favorite time of day."

He caught Theresa's eye, and she put her hand over her mouth to hide a smile. "I rest my case," he said.

"I thought maybe this morning after breakfast Ken could show you the new pasture we bought this spring," Kristen said as she arranged slices of bread on the toaster oven rack. "Theresa and I can hit the shops in Wimberley. We can all meet back here for lunch and then maybe we could go riding."

"Whoa! Stop!" Kyle held up his hand. "I thought I'd take Theresa on a tour of the ranch this morning. Alone."

Kristen deflated, her bubbly mood burst. "But I want you to see all the improvements we've made. And you don't care about shopping." She turned to Theresa. "Wimberley has some of the most wonderful boutiques and antique stores. I know you'd love it."

Theresa was always up for shopping. And visiting Wimberley would probably be fun—with anyone but Kristen.

"We came here this weekend to relax, just the two of us," he said. "Don't go making elaborate plans."

"I just thought it would be fun." Kristen regained her composure somewhat. "We don't see near enough of you these days. Theresa has a brother. I'm sure she understands."

Kyle's expression softened. "Maybe this afternoon we could go riding."

Theresa frowned. Climbing on the back of some big beast wasn't her idea of fun. And until Kristen had pressed her point, it hadn't been what Kyle had in mind, either. Suddenly the kitchen was entirely too stuffy for her. "I think I'll go outside and get some fresh air," she said, and before anyone could stop her, she left.

KYLE CAUGHT UP WITH THERESA just outside the horse corral. He didn't blame her for bugging out like that. Kristen could be pretty hard to take when you didn't know her very well. If only the guesthouse had been empty the way he'd planned. He wouldn't have to deal with all this. As it was, Theresa was probably wondering why he'd bothered bringing her up here this weekend.

He was wondering that himself. "I'm sorry about all that," he said, stopping outside the gate to the horse corral. "When I've been away for a while, I forget how she is."

Her eyes on his were steady. "If you really want her to stop trying to run your life, you're going to have to sit her down and tell her exactly how you feel."

"I've done that! She doesn't listen."

"That's because you've been too nice."

"So you're suggesting I deliberately hurt her feelings?"

"That might be what it takes to get her to really pay attention."

"I don't see any reason to start a family feud."

"What you see as keeping the peace, she sees as going along with her plans."

"I've learned to ignore her. Why can't you?"

She looked away, arms crossed over her breasts. She was so beautiful. And so infuriating. Why did the women in his life drive him crazy? "Why do you care, anyway?" he asked. "What difference does it make to you?"

She opened her mouth to speak and he held his breath. So he'd been right—she *did* care. He wasn't the only one who'd gotten into this over his head.

But then she clamped her mouth shut again and shook her head. "You're right. It's none of my business. You do whatever you think you have to do." She turned away and stared out over the corral railing.

It wasn't the answer he wanted, but clearly it was the only one he was going to get. Fine. He could play it cool. Ignore these crazy feelings she stirred in him until he either couldn't keep them inside anymore or they went away. Over the years he'd gotten pretty good at acting a part, whether it was all-American cowboy or good-timing playboy. People saw what they wanted to see, anyway.

The difference with Theresa was, he'd been sure up until now that with her at least he could always show his true self.

THERESA WAS RELIEVED WHEN Kyle didn't press her further for an answer to his question. When he suggested he show her around the ranch, she eagerly agreed. Call her a coward, but she wasn't ready to look any closer at her feelings for this man.

And anyway, what if she gave the wrong answer, one he didn't want to hear? She still had almost two whole days stuck here with him. Better to keep things light and enjoy themselves than risk disaster by saying something she shouldn't.

"If you're going to ride this afternoon, you might as well meet the horses first." He opened the corral gate and ushered her in.

She glanced at the horses that stood along the fence at the opposite end of the corral and kept close to Kyle. "I've never been around horses much," she said, determined not to let him see her nervousness.

"Just remember you're smarter than they are." He took her arm and led her toward the trio of animals.

"But they're bigger than I am," she muttered.

He smiled but said nothing. Just seeing that smile made her relax a little. After all, if he wasn't afraid, why should she be?

Up close, the horses were even bigger. One snorted, peeling back rubbery lips to show enormous teeth right at her eye level. She leaned away from it, but Kyle took her hand in his and drew her closer. "I want you to meet Rocket Man. One of the best calf-roping horses on the circuit today." He scratched behind the big animal's ear. "We've won a lot of money together, haven't we, pard?"

The horse twitched its ears, then fixed intelligent toffee-colored eyes on Theresa. "Rocket Man?" She laughed at the name.

"It's officially Dandy's Bottle Rocket, but he's always been the Rocket Man to me." He turned fond eyes to the horse again.

His obvious affection for the animal touched her. "How long have you had him?" she asked.

"About six years now." He patted the horse's neck. "We're both getting a little long in the tooth for competition, but I hate the thought of giving him up and getting a new partner."

"Would you sell him?"

He shook his head. "Nah. He'll retire here. Kelly exercises him for me and I pay for his feed. It's a good setup for him." He gave the horse a last pat, then led her to another horse, one with a dark brown coat and black mane and tail. "This is Sweet Pea. He's the oldest one in the bunch, real gentle. He's probably the one you'll ride."

Sweet Pea watched her with calm, intelligent eyes as she smoothed her hand down his velvety nose. She smiled. "He *is* sweet."

He laughed and slipped his arm around her waist. "So are you." He rested his chin on her shoulder as he hugged her from behind. "Hey, I'm sorry if I put you on the spot back there. I invited you up here this weekend to have fun, not to get involved in my family soap opera."

"It's okay." She snuggled closer, a familiar warmth spreading through her. He must have felt it, too, since the ridge in the front of his jeans grew more pronounced against her backside.

"Mmm." He kissed her neck above her shirt collar, his warm lips teasing a spark of arousal into a slow burn. "Are you still wondering what it would be like to have a real roll in the hay?"

"Before breakfast?" she teased.

"It's a great way to work up an appetite." He slid his hands up to cover her breasts, his mouth still sending delicious sensations all along her neck.

"I thought you said hay was scratchy." Not that she wasn't warming up to the idea, but it never hurt to play a little hard to get.

"I know where they keep the blankets." He pinched her nipples lightly, and she was afraid her knees might buckle at any moment.

"A-all right," she gasped.

He grabbed her hand and tugged her into the barn and over to a ladder. "You climb on up and I'll get the blanket." He patted her backside, then ducked into an empty stall.

Keeping her eye out for spiders, mice or other wildlife,

she slowly climbed the ladder into the loft. The area was surprisingly clean, smelling of sweet hay and oats. In less than a minute, Kyle joined her, a gray-and-black blanket draped over his shoulder.

"Hope you're not allergic to wool," he said, tossing the blanket to her.

"Not that I know of." She spread the coverlet out on a pile of loose hay and settled back on it. "It's pretty comfortable."

"I promise to make it feel even better." He crawled toward her on his hands and knees, both the posture and the naked lust in his eyes speaking to some primitive emotion within her. She felt wild and wanton and free of both inhibitions and expectations.

"Come here." She beckoned with one finger as she began to unfasten her blouse with her other hand. "I've got something for you."

"Mmm, very nice." He reached her and lowered his head to kiss her exposed cleavage, following the path of her hand with his mouth. He unsnapped her bra and smiled down at her naked breasts. "Very nice indeed."

She arched up off the blanket when his mouth closed around her nipple, desire jolting through her. All the doubts and confused feelings that had plagued her, all the edginess she'd been feeling these past few days, coalesced into a fierce need. This was what she wanted, what she needed—this reminder that whatever old fears her brain put in her way, her heart and body seemed to know that whenever she was with *this* man, things would be all right. She didn't have to be afraid of anything or hide anything from him. That knowledge was a powerful aphrodisiac, sharpening her desire to an exquisite edge.

He transferred his attention to her other breast, and she reached for the zipper of his jeans, anxious to feel him in her hand. She hoped he'd had the foresight to slip a condom into his pants before they'd left the house. But even if he hadn't, they could still enjoy themselves....

"Kyle? Theresa? Breakfast is ready!"

13

THEY BOTH FROZE, HIS LIPS pressed against her breast, her fingers gripping his zipper. "She'll go away in a minute when we don't answer," he whispered.

She nodded and held her breath, listening.

"Kyle! Breakfast is waiting." Instead of moving away, the voice moved closer. The door of the barn creaked as it opened.

Kyle stifled a groan. Theresa pushed him off her and struggled to do up her blouse. The last thing she wanted was for Kristen to find them like this. "Kyle? Are you in here?"

Their eyes met, the frustration she felt clearly telegraphed in his expression. They could hear Kristen moving around below them. "Kyle, I don't have time to play games," Kristen said. "Kelly said he thought he saw you come in here. Breakfast is waiting."

It sounded as if she was almost at the bottom of the ladder now. He scowled, then put a finger to his lips.

Theresa nodded, and he eased away from her toward the ladder. At the last minute, he reached out and tugged the blanket from beneath her. She raised her hips and let him take it, curious what part the prop would play.

She watched him disappear down the ladder, then finished buttoning up her shirt.

"There you are! Didn't you hear me calling you? Where's Theresa?"

"I think she walked on down to the creek."

"What are you doing in the hayloft then?"

"I was looking for this blanket. I thought I might persuade Theresa to put it to good use on the creek bank."

She covered her mouth with her hand to stifle a laugh, imagining the leer that no doubt accompanied Kyle's words.

"Kyle!" Kristen apparently didn't find the suggestion very amusing. "It's not even eight o'clock."

"Don't tell me you've never enjoyed a little vitamin L to start your day off right."

She ignored his teasing. "What's that blanket doing up in the loft anyway?"

"I don't know. I thought maybe you and Ken sneaked up here for a little nooky away from the kids."

"I have four children and a ranch to run. I don't have time to be sneaking away for nooky."

"You ought to try it sometime. It would improve your disposition."

"There's nothing wrong with my disposition."

"Except you've been fussing at me practically ever since I pulled into the driveway."

"Only because I love you and I worry about you."

"There's nothing to worry about. I'm doing just fine."

"I might believe that if you showed any signs of settling down, but you don't."

"I brought a woman home to meet you. That ought to make you happy."

"Ha!" The disdain in that one syllable surprised Theresa. She inched closer to the edge of the loft and looked down. She couldn't see Kyle and only glimpsed Kristen's profile. She was frowning, arms crossed at her waist as she contemplated her brother. "You and I both know Theresa isn't your type. She's just another phase you're going through, like that time you started dressing all preppy. Or when you bought that land in Austin and told us you were going to build a house and live out there."

"How do you know that?"

"Because that's the way you are. You do this stuff to get a rise out of everyone. I know you. Now come on. I don't have time to stand here all day talking. Go get Theresa and come to breakfast."

She walked out of sight, and Theresa scooted back away from the edge of the loft. Her heart was pounding and she felt cold and hollow inside. So Kristen thought she was just another "phase" for Kyle. Something meant to shake them up, like his previous attempts to do so. Of course! She'd known this all along, but it hadn't mattered until she'd made the mistake of falling in love with the man.

She pressed the heels of her hands to her eyes, swallowing the knot of emotion stuck in her throat. Hadn't she known this would happen? Get attached to something you couldn't have and you'd only end up disappointed in the end. It had been true when she was ten and wanted the doll her foster sister let her play with, and when she was fourteen and had her heart set on being adopted by the Rodgers family, and when she was nineteen and gave her heart away to a married man.

And now she'd let down her guard for a rodeo Romeo who didn't have a job or a real home or any idea of what he wanted out of life. All he'd promised her was a good time, and she'd screwed it all up by expecting more.

"Hey, you okay?"

She straightened and opened her eyes, blinking at him. "Okay? Yeah, sure. Just…a bit of a headache." Somehow she dredged up a weak smile. "Maybe I *am* allergic to wool."

"Guess you heard all that." His earlier charm was gone, replaced by a tired expression. His shoulders slumped, and for the first time she noticed the shadows beneath his eyes.

She nodded and scooted toward him. "Your sister is just the type who worries," she said. "Don't let it get you down."

"I can live with the worrying," he said. "It's her being so sure she knows what I'm like—when she doesn't know anything at all—that makes me furious." He shook his head. "She keeps bringing up that preppy stuff, but I was just a kid when that happened. And the only reason I haven't built a house on my place by the lake is that I don't have the money yet."

And what about me? she thought but didn't dare ask. The fact that he hadn't mentioned her himself said all she needed to know. Apparently Kristen had been right about that one.

"Let's go get some breakfast," she said, and stepped on to the first rung of the ladder.

She followed him down and across the corral to the house. So much for vitamin L. She thought she'd learned to live with that particular deficiency, but it was a lot harder to give it up when you thought you'd had it in your hands.

AN AFTERNOON OF HORSEBACK riding proved to Theresa that she was not meant to be a cowgirl. While the others ambled up hills and raced across pastures, she lagged behind, alternately trying to coax Sweet Pea into moving faster than a slow plod, and hanging on for dear life when he settled into a bone-jarring trot. By the time they came back to the ranch house, she was hot, dusty and irritable, and her butt, thighs and knees ached.

"I guess we might have overdid it for your first day," Kristen said as she watched Theresa make her way gingerly up the front steps. "Why don't you take a hot bath before supper? That'll make you feel a lot better, I'm sure."

"Thanks. I think I will." Kristen's concern sounded genuine, but maybe that was only because she didn't consider Theresa a real threat to her plans for Kyle. After all, Theresa was just a "phase." As soon as Kristen could make him see the error of his ways, her brother would settle down with her and her family on the ranch and everything would be peachy keen.

It was enough to make Theresa gag. "Damn right, I don't belong here," she muttered as she stripped off her clothes in the guest bath. "If Kyle does decide to one day settle down here on the lone prairie, it's a good thing I didn't start planning a future with him."

She lowered herself into the steaming water and closed her eyes, trying to shut out memories of that interlude in the hayloft, when she'd been so sure Kyle was the man for her.

But as soon as she'd chased away those thoughts, other images flashed in her mind—Kyle laughing with her at the tattoo shop, Kyle seated across from her on the riverboat, Kyle doing an exaggerated bump and grind, wearing only chaps and his Stetson.

She sank lower in the water and sighed. She might not fit into his world here at the ranch, but he'd sure looked at home in her world back in Austin.

Still, his heart was obviously here. Otherwise he would have worked harder to convince Kristen he didn't want to be a partner with her and Ken in running the place. And after all, this was his family home, a place he was linked to by all those ranching ancestors. Even someone like her, who'd never had any kind of real home, could imagine how powerful that pull was. For all her annoying bossiness, Kristen was probably right—when Kyle matured more and got over the wanderlust that plagued him, he'd come back to his roots and his upbringing.

When she'd soaked so long the water was cool and her fingers and toes were as wrinkled as unironed cotton, she dried off and went into her bedroom and searched through her suitcase for something to wear.

She was pawing through the folded jeans and shirts when her hand brushed the plastic covering over the white eyelet-trimmed dress she'd packed at the bottom of the case. She'd never worn the dress. It was entirely too frilly and romantic for her wardrobe, and she'd only bought it on a dare when she and Zach's girlfriend, Jen, had been out shopping one day. She couldn't imagine what had possessed her to bring it on this trip, except that obviously silly thoughts of love and romance had clouded her thinking. She moved a pair of jeans over to hide the dress once more, and her eyes landed on the red satin bustier. She'd put that in, along with red satin tap pants and a pair of strappy red heels, with the idea of playing dress up for Kyle when they were alone one evening.

Fat chance of that happening now. She fingered the bustier and smiled at the positively evil idea that popped into her head. Why not wear the bustier tonight—to dinner? She'd clear up any doubts anyone had about her being anything more than another one of Kyle's wild phases and she'd tease him a little with the knowledge of all he was missing as long as Kristen choreographed the weekend.

"ARE YOU SURE SHE HASN'T fallen asleep or something?" Kristen asked Kyle as they all sat around the dinner table waiting for Theresa. "Maybe I should go up and check on her."

"I stopped by on my way down and told her dinner was ready. She told me she was almost ready."

"And was she? Almost ready I mean?"

"I guess so." He frowned. "She wouldn't open the door, but she sounded fine." In fact she'd sounded a lot more cheerful than she had earlier. He could tell she hadn't had much fun on their ride this afternoon and he blamed himself. He'd been so intent on getting Ken alone to talk about an idea he'd had about the ranch that he hadn't really noticed Theresa falling behind until it was too late. By the time he went back for her, she would hardly speak to him. And before he could apologize, Kristen had joined them, irritatingly cheerful and looking like the former barrel racer she was; perfectly at ease on a horse, while Theresa had looked decidedly uncomfortable.

He checked his watch. At least twenty minutes had passed since he'd stopped by Theresa's room. The fried chicken Kristen had made was getting cold. Maybe something was wrong.

He pushed back his chair, intending to go upstairs and check on her, when he heard her call from the next room. "I'm sorry I kept everyone waiting. Everything took longer than I expected."

He turned in time to watch her come through the doorway, and choked back a gasp.

"Damn!"

It wasn't Kyle who'd uttered the word but Ken, whose eyes looked two sizes larger as he stared at Theresa.

The disheveled, limping woman who'd staggered up the stairs two hours before had transformed herself into a red-hot femme fatale in red stiletto heels, skintight black leather pants and the red satin top she'd worn the night they'd had dinner on the riverboat—a top that revealed more than it covered. Kyle's gaze fixed on the swell of her breasts above the satin and he found himself wondering how far she'd have to lean over before she popped right out of there.

He began to feel dizzy and thought it might be because all the blood in his body had rushed straight to his groin, and then he realized he'd been holding his breath. He let it out in a rush as Theresa stopped beside his chair.

Just in time, he stood and pulled her chair out for her, aware of every eye in the room on them.

"Wow, you look amazing!" Kelly was the first to put thoughts into words. The compliment earned him a dazzling smile from Theresa.

"Thank you," she said as she spread her napkin into her lap. "After playing cowgirl all afternoon, I felt like dressing up."

She swept her hair back over her shoulder, a half dozen silver bracelets jangling as she moved. Kyle caught a whiff of her perfume, spicy and erotic, and was glad of the napkin spread over his lap that hid his reaction.

Kristen was the only one not staring at Theresa. "Ken, why don't you go ahead and say grace?"

Somehow Kyle managed to hold it together, even when Ken thanked the Lord for "all this bounty at our table."

He tried to concentrate on his plate, though every sense was fully aware of the woman beside him. Ken continued to grin at Theresa, while Kristen made attempts at conversation, asking the girls and Kelly about their day at camp and commenting at length on the hot, dry weather.

"This dinner is delicious," Theresa said. "I don't know when I've eaten anything so good." When she delicately licked chicken grease from her fingers, Kyle stifled a groan. Ken began coughing and reached for his tea.

Kristen smiled weakly. "Thank you. I like to cook. I guess when you enjoy something, it's easy to be good at it."

"I couldn't agree more." She sent Kyle a smoldering look, which made him think of things Theresa enjoyed—things she was very good at.

He fixed his gaze on his plate, but the food couldn't satisfy the particular appetite Theresa had awakened.

"Before y'all make any plans for tomorrow, I wanted to let you know we've got a few people coming over."

Kristen spoke matter-of-factly, but Kyle could see nothing innocent in this announcement. "I thought I told you not to schedule anything else for us," he said.

"I didn't plan this. Not exactly." She wiped her fingers on her napkin. "When I mentioned you were coming to visit, a few people said they wanted to stop by and say hello. Then I guess word got around and a few more people called." She dropped the crumpled napkin beside her plate. "The next thing I knew, we were having a barbecue."

He groaned and glanced at Theresa. She looked wary. "Will there be a lot of people here?" she asked.

"Oh, just a few neighbors and friends. Not more than thirty or so."

Great. Thirty local yokels to stare at crazy Kyle Cameron and his tattooed girlfriend. He could hear the gossip mill shifting into overdrive already. "We'll leave early if it gets too hectic," he said. He meant the words as reassurance for Theresa—and as a warning for Kristen.

He'd about had it with his sister always running the show. She wasn't going to like it one bit when he started doing things his way, but that was too bad.

At last the meal was over and he saw his chance.

"Why don't we play games in the family room," Kristen said as Kim and Kelly cleared the table. She nudged Kyle. "I might even let you win a game of Clue."

"I don't think so." He grabbed Theresa's hand. "Theresa and I are going to take a walk."

"We are?" Theresa looked down at her sexy high heels. "I'm not really dressed for hiking."

"Don't worry, we won't go far." He tugged her toward the door.

"What a good idea," Kristen said. "We could all use the exercise, and it's a nice night."

Ken put his arm around his wife's shoulders. "I think he means he and Theresa are going for a walk *alone*." He grinned at Kyle. "Y'all have a good time. We'll stay here and hold down the fort."

They escaped the house at last. Kyle took Theresa's hand and led the way down the drive, away from the house. The moon was almost full and the white caliche drive was bright as a runway.

When they'd rounded the first bend in the drive, out of

sight of the ranch house, Theresa stopped. "You're going to have to walk slower or I'll twist an ankle in these shoes."

He looked her up and down. "So what's with the sexpot getup?"

She adjusted the thin shoulder strap of her top. "Maybe I just felt like dressing up."

"If you're trying to shock my sister, I'd say you've succeeded."

"I wasn't trying to shock her." She shrugged. "Not much, anyway."

"Then why the outfit?"

Her expression turned sultry. "Don't you like it?"

In answer, he pulled her tight against his chest and covered her lips in a searing kiss. By the time he raised his head, they were both out of breath. "What do you think?"

She smoothed her hands across his chest, up to his shoulders, and ground her pelvis against his. "I think you like it."

"I have some good memories of this outfit." He put his hands at her waist, holding her still. "Don't distract me. Answer my question."

The seductive expression vanished, and she took a step away from him. "I dressed this way because this is the real me." She put her hands on her hips, as if daring him to disagree with her. "I like sexy clothes. I like showing off my body. I'm not a cowgirl and never will be."

He nodded. "I think everyone here realizes that."

"Do they? Do you?"

"Hell, yes, I do." He took a step toward her, but she moved back, keeping him at arm's length. "That's one of the reasons I like you."

"Right." She turned and walked away, little puffs of caliche rising each time her heels struck the ground.

In three long strides, he caught up with her and grabbed her by the arm, whirling her around to face him. "What is with you?" he demanded. "Why are you acting all pissed off at me?"

Some of the stiffness went out of her shoulders. "I'm not pissed off at you. I'm just feeling, I don't know, a little out of place." Her eyes met his, the confusion in them in sharp contrast to her in-your-face attire. "I needed to remind myself—and everyone else—what I'm really like."

He smoothed his hand down her arm, straining to understand what this conversation was really about. "If this has anything to do with the horseback riding this afternoon, I'm sorry about that. I know you didn't have a good time."

She shrugged. "Everyone else did. No reason for me to spoil y'all's fun."

"I should have put my foot down and told Kristen we wouldn't go. I should have gone off somewhere with you, the way I've wanted to all weekend."

She looked away. "I know it's hard for you to say no to her. And I know she's your only relative and—"

"No." He squeezed her shoulder, interrupting her. "I've been thinking about what you said earlier—about how I'm too quick to give in to her, to go along."

She shook her head. "It wasn't any of my bus—"

"No. You were right. I've been lazy. But that's going to change. From now on I'm going to do what I want, even if other people don't like it."

"What do you want?" She faced him and looked into his eyes, trapping him.

He forced himself not to look away—didn't think he could if he tried. She had the most amazing eyes, dark and expressive, full of sadness and sympathy and a thousand other emotions he didn't even understand yet. He could fall into those eyes and forget everything else. There was so much he wanted to tell her, but all those words could wait for later. Right now, he wanted to speak without words, to show her what he was feeling instead of trying to tell her.

"I want this."

His kiss was gentle, a soft brush of his lips that silently asked permission for more. She responded by slipping her arms around him and pulling him closer, her mouth parting slightly, her tongue slipping between his teeth.

Her body was warm and yielding against his, her soft curves conforming to him as he pressed his palm against the small of her back and urged her closer still. He'd been hot for her off and on all day, ever since their interrupted make-out session in the loft. He didn't want to wait any longer.

He broke the kiss and stared down into her eyes. Her slightly glazed look testified to her own arousal. "Wanna go skinny-dipping?" he asked.

She blinked. "Now? Where?"

"I know the perfect place." He took her hand and tugged her off the drive, toward the shortcut through the woods to a spot they jokingly referred to as the "family swimming pool." They'd taken only a few steps when she stumbled, muttering curses.

"Hold on." He put his arm around her to steady her, then bent and tugged the shoe off first one foot, then the other. Then he tossed them into the darkness.

"Kyle! Those sandals cost over a hundred dollars!"

"They'll still be there in the morning. It's not like anybody's going to come out here and carry them off."

"If they're not, you owe me a pair of shoes."

"It'll be worth it to get you to that creek before we both have a meltdown."

Barefoot, she was able to move faster, and a few minutes later they emerged from the cut in the woods onto the creek bank. A bend in the watercourse had thrown up a natural sandy beach, and hundred-year-old live oaks extended massive limbs to shade the water and provide the perfect place for rope swings and diving platforms.

"It's really dark," she said softly, lowering her voice to match their hushed surroundings.

"Uh-huh." He drew her close once more and nipped at the corner of her mouth. "Dark and private. This time of year the water's warm, too." He squeezed her breast.

She glanced toward the creek. "Aren't there snakes?"

"No snakes." He kissed her neck. Her skin was soft and she tasted both sweet and salty.

"Are you sure?"

"I'm sure. The bobcats keep them away."

"Bobcats!" Her voice rose.

He laughed. "Don't worry. They live around here but they're shy. They won't come around people."

"Maybe they wouldn't like us being here." She tugged his head up, forcing him to pay attention. "I'm a city girl. I'm not used to wild animals."

"Darlin', the only wild animal you need to be worried about right now is me." He stripped off his cast, then found the hooks that fastened her top and began to release them one by one. In the dimness, he could barely make out the shape of her breasts, the nipples dark circles in the shadows. He shaped his hands to her, feeling the weight and roundness of her, his erection beginning to throb. He'd better slow things down or they'd get out of hand in a hurry.

"Still nervous?" he asked.

She nodded. "A little. But…turned on, too." She reached for his belt buckle.

He grinned. "How about if we both get naked and I carry you into the water? That way you'll be safe."

"Safe from everything but you!"

"That's the idea, isn't it?" He lowered the zipper of her pants and slipped his hand beneath the silk of her underwear.

Laughing, she darted away and quickly stripped out of the rest of her clothes. He did the same, draping his shirt and pants over nearby bushes. When they were kids, clothes draped on those bushes had served as a warning for girls to keep out, though as he'd gotten older, the secret fantasy had always been for the girls to come and spy on him and his friends. But if any ever had, they'd kept quiet about it.

He reached for her hand. "You ready?"

"I guess so." She moved into his arms. "But if there are any snakes, I'll never forgive you."

"No snakes," he said, leading her into the water. "Only a certain sea monster looking for a warm dark cave to explore."

She groaned. "That's really bad, you know that?"

"I didn't say I was a poet, darlin'. But I'm a pretty good dancer."

"So you've told me."

They were up to their waists in the water now. As he'd promised, it wasn't cold but warm and silken against her skin. He smoothed his hands along her hips and she pressed her palm to his chest, enjoying the feel of both water and skin, her senses heightened by the open air and darkness.

"Seems to me you've liked the dancing we've done so far," he said.

"Oh, yeah. I've liked it. I've liked it a lot."

He took her hand and led her farther out to where her feet no longer touched bottom. She started to tread water, and he dived beneath the surface. She felt him glide past her and then he was behind her, his hands on her breasts, his body pressed to hers. The warm water wrapped around them.

"Did you bring other women here to do this?" she asked.

His breath was warm against her neck. "I'm probably ruining my reputation here, but no. The summer of my junior year in high school, I spent a lot of time trying to persuade Analise Shroeder to come out here with me, but she told me if we got caught, her brothers would kill me. She had three older brothers who had all earned football scholarships to Texas A&M, so I decided it wasn't worth the risk, even to see Analise naked." He flicked her nipples with his thumbs, sending ripples out around them and deeper ripples of sensation through her. "I don't think it would have been half as nice as being here with you right now."

"That's right. My brother isn't going to kill you. He'd probably shake your hand instead." Truly, Zach would be pleased to see her happy in a relationship, even if the happiness was only temporary.

"And I think a man has to have a few years on him to truly appreciate women." She turned and his eyes met hers. "Everything about women." He cradled the back of her head in his hand. "They say good sex is in the brain as much as the body."

"So you think I have a sexy brain?" The idea pleased her.

"Woman, you have an amazing brain to go with this amazing body." He turned her around to face him and his lips closed over hers. She put her whole self into the kiss. Knowing that even when they were making love he thought about more than just her body moved her. She'd spent a lot of years convincing herself she was only interested in the physical side of a man/woman relationship, and in no time at all he'd proved her a liar.

She ought to hate him for that but here, with no walls to hide behind and no light but that of the moon filtered through trees, she looked into his eyes and knew she'd fallen in love with Kyle Cameron. She couldn't lie to herself anymore about that one.

But love hadn't robbed her of all her good sense, either. She wasn't about to bare her soul along with her body and take the hurt that confession was bound to bring. There was no reason for her and Kyle to be together in the long run, so she'd nurse her wounds alone later and make the most of the here and now. The thought added an urgency to her passion and made her forget her nervousness about snakes and wild animals and the darkness. She was Eve seducing Adam, with no one and nothing to stop her.

Smiling, she took his hand and guided it down until he covered her sex. He squeezed gently. "Feeling brave?" he asked.

"Feeling like I can't wait for you any longer." She gripped his shoulders and wrapped her legs around his waist, the water helping to support her.

He widened his stance, steadying them both. "Believe

me, I know the feeling," he said and arched against her, his erection hard and hot against her clit.

"Then why don't you come inside and stay a while?" She trailed her fingers along his chest.

"Because you're not ready~yet." He bent and suckled first one nipple, then the other, every pull of his lips sending a new tremor through her.

"H-how do you know if…if I'm ready or…or not?" she gasped.

"Because when I slide into you, I want you so wet and aching that you see stars from the first stroke." He slid his hands between them and buried two fingers in her. She tightened around him, a little moan escaping her.

"Stars?" she asked.

His thumb flicked across her clit. "You'll see stars and feel thunderbolts." He drove his fingers deeper, sending a spasm of arousal deep into her womb. She fought to clench her thighs together, but with her legs wrapped around him it was impossible. She was trapped, completely vulnerable, the sensation of lapping water, probing fingers, stroking thumb and the warm caress of his mouth on her breast overwhelming her. She began to tremble, quaking with desire. He increased the tempo of his stroking and murmured against her breast. "Come on, baby. Tell me how much you love it. No one can hear you out here."

She bit his shoulder to muffle her scream, some shadow of awareness not believing that someone wouldn't come running to investigate a shout. Her climax rocketed through her, and she clung to him with her legs and arms, supported by him and the water.

She didn't know how long they stood there like that before he pushed her gently away. She let her legs slip from around him as he towed her toward shore. When her feet touched the gravelly creek bottom, she must have moaned her regret, because he bent and kissed the side of her mouth. "I'm not going anywhere," he said. "It's just my turn now."

While she watched, still dazed, he waded to the bank and retrieved his jeans. Moonlight glinted on a familiar foil packet as he slipped it from his pocket. Laughter bubbled in her throat. "I can't believe you came prepared," she said. "Did you plan this?"

"Not plan, exactly." He tore open the packet and sheathed himself. "But I've been carrying this around with me all day." He started toward her once more. "I was determined to get you alone sometime."

He put his hands on her hips, his penis nudging between her thighs. "Think you can wrap your legs around me like that again?"

She laughed. "I think I can manage."

The position didn't afford the opportunity for much movement, but that in itself gave the moment an added intensity. Facing each other in the moonlight, literally wrapped around each other, they looked into one another's eyes. She brushed the hair back from his forehead and kissed the bridge of his nose, thinking how she would never tire of looking at a man who gazed at her with such tenderness.

He clutched her bottom and fit himself deeper into her. Gentle waves lapped around them with each shallow thrust. From time to time they stilled and indulged in long, deep kisses, their tongues as entwined as their limbs. And then they would begin to move again. She felt the tension within her begin to build and saw the same urgency in his eyes.

He thrust deeper now, the water slapping against her back as he moved faster, harder. She dug her fingernails into the skin of his shoulder and closed her eyes against the heat spreading through her. The light that exploded behind her eyes as she came was very like stars, and when he shouted his release, she wondered if he'd felt the lightning.

Spent and shaky, he withdrew from her and helped her to stand. He kissed her forehead and then her eyes, like a benediction. "Thank you," he whispered.

"For what?" She smiled. "I ought to thank you for bringing me here. The water and the moonlight—it's like a dream."

"You're a dream," he said. "I—"

She put her fingers over his lips, silencing him. "Don't say anything. I don't want any words cluttering up the wonderful way this feels."

He hesitated, then nodded. "All right. No more talking. Not tonight. But we'll talk soon."

She turned away, heading for the bank. She would put off talking as long as she could. Talking could lead to discussing the different directions they were headed. She wanted to avoid that conversation as long as possible.

14

WHEN THERESA WOKE SUNDAY morning, she was startled to find it was after nine o'clock. The K clan would have finished breakfast hours ago. Yawning, she shoved herself into a sitting position and squinted in the bright light streaming through the window. Early to bed and early to rise might make these ranchers healthy and wise, but she'd settle for late nights and sleeping in any day. And with the barbecue today, she needed all the energy she could muster to meet Kyle's friends and neighbors.

She went to the bathroom and brushed her teeth and was standing in front of the mirror combing out her hair when she heard a knock on the door. She grabbed her robe from the hook behind the door and slipped into it, checked in the mirror to make sure she was presentable, then called, "Come in."

The door creaked open and Kim entered carrying a tray in both hands. "Good morning," she said. "Mama thought you might want some coffee."

Steam curled from the oversize mug that sat next to a plate of the most delectable-looking coffee cake. A glass of orange juice completed the offerings. Guilt over every bitchy thought she'd had about Kyle's sister pinched at Theresa. "That looks wonderful," she said, hurrying to take the tray from the girl.

"I brought you these, too." Kim held up a pair of red high-heeled sandals.

Theresa blushed. "Where did she find those?" she asked, remembering how Kyle had hurled them into the darkness.

"They were in the front yard this morning when I went out to get the paper." Kim sat on the edge of the bed. "What were they doing out there?"

"When your uncle Kyle and I went for a walk, they were slowing me down, so he made me take them off and he tossed them on the grass. I guess we forgot to go back for them." She took a long drink of coffee, hoping the girl didn't notice how red her face was bound to be. After the creek, she'd been doing well to remember her name, much less a pair of uncomfortable shoes.

"They're really pretty shoes." Kim ran her finger over the ankle strap of one of them. "But they do look like they'd be hard to walk in."

"They are. Not very practical for the country." She took a bite of coffee cake and all but moaned. "Your mother sure is a good cook," she said.

"She's in the kitchen right now fixing all kinds of things for the barbecue."

Theresa's stomach gave a nervous flutter. "Do you know the people coming to this barbecue?" she asked.

Kim shrugged. "I know most of them. Most of the neighbors will be here and people from town. But it's not like at roundup, when a couple hundred folks might show up to help. There'll probably only be a few dozen today."

"A few dozen sounds like a lot of people to me." *Thirty* had sounded like a lot when Kristen had named the number last night. The guest list apparently kept growing. She took another drink of coffee. And what would they all think of Kyle's city girlfriend? It annoyed her that she even cared. After all, what did a bunch of strangers' opinions matter to her?

But Kyle's opinion did matter, and for his sake she wanted to make a good impression. "Where is your uncle right now?" she asked.

"He and Daddy are out by the cooker watching the brisket." Kim made a face. "It doesn't really need watching, but they stand out there and talk and pretend they're working. Mostly I think they do it so Mama won't think they're not busy and start bossing them around."

Theresa stifled laughter, imagining the two men hiding out from Kristen.

"So where did you and Uncle Kyle go on your walk last night?"

"Oh, we went down to the creek."

"Did you go swimming?"

Coffee sloshed in the cup as Theresa set it down hard on the dresser. "Wh-what makes you say that?"

Kim shrugged. "Nobody goes to the creek except to swim or fish, and I never heard of anybody fishing in the dark."

She laughed at the logic, but wasn't about to admit guilt. "Kyle wanted to show me the creek." That was no lie, at least. He'd shown her the creek and a lot more. She felt warm and dreamy at the memory.

"You have such cool clothes. What are you going to wear to the barbecue today?"

Kim's question snapped Theresa out of her daydream. "I don't know. What do you think I should wear?"

"Wear your leather pants. Nobody around here wears

leather pants." Kim tilted her head to one side. "My dad sometimes wears leather chaps, but those don't really count." She giggled. "When he wears them, Mama tells him he has a cute butt."

Theresa remembered Kyle in his chaps. Yes, they did do a lot for a man's butt…. She shook her head. "I've already worn my leather pants twice this weekend. Besides, this barbecue is outside, isn't it? I need something cooler."

"You could wear jeans. That's what most people wear." Her expression became animated and she sat up straighter. "I know. Wear a dress. Some of the women wear sundresses. You'd be cool and I bet you'd look really pretty, too."

"I don't know. I don't usually wear dresses." She thought of the eyelet-lace number she'd packed on a whim. She'd never actually worn the dress. At least not in public.

"Did you bring a dress? Or maybe you could wear one of Mama's." She frowned at Theresa's chest. "Though you're bigger in front than she is, but maybe she has something stretchy."

"I brought one dress." She went over to her suitcase and unearthed the white dress.

"Wow! It's gorgeous!" Kim slid off the bed and stood close to Theresa, hands behind her back as if she was afraid of touching all that lace. "That would be perfect."

"You don't think it's too dressy?" Theresa frowned at the eyelet panels running under the arms and down the sides of the skirt.

"No, it looks really summery and pretty. You'd have to be careful not to get barbecue sauce on it, though."

"I think I could do that." For one thing, if she wore this dress, she'd be too nervous and self-conscious to eat. But it might be fun to show Kyle that she could be as feminine and frilly as the next gal—when she felt like it.

"You should wear it," Kim said.

She nodded. "All right, I think I will."

"Great. I'll go get the iron so you can touch it up. And Mama has some white flowers in the back flower bed that would look awesome in your hair."

"I don't know about the flowers…." But the girl had already left the room, eager to help transform her own personal Cinderella. Theresa sat on the end of the bed and stared at the dress. She only hoped she didn't end up looking like a fool by the time the day was over.

WHEN THERESA DIDN'T COME down for breakfast, Kristen had wanted to send one of the girls upstairs to wake her, but Kyle had talked her out of it. "Let her sleep," he said. "This is supposed to be a vacation for her."

"I don't want her to miss breakfast," Kristen said.

"You can save something for her for later," he said. "It'll be all right."

Though he missed having her seated next to him, he welcomed the chance to finish the discussion he'd started yesterday with Ken about the ranch. Kristen would be fit to be tied when she found out what he'd been up to, but Ken had promised she'd come around. "I think it's a real good thing you're doing," he'd told Kyle yesterday. "It's a big step, but in the end, I think it'll be best for all of us."

Would Theresa think so, too? He'd wanted to tell her everything last night, but decided against it. She hadn't wanted to spoil their mood with words, and he'd told himself it would be better to wait until everything was settled before he made his big announcement. He still wasn't sure how she was going to take the news. And maybe he ought to tell Kristen first, anyway.

But when guests started arriving and he still hadn't seen Theresa, he began to get a little worried. He stopped Kim on her way up the stairs. "Maybe you'd better go check on Theresa for me," he said. "Make sure she isn't sick."

"She's fine." Kim held up the iron she was carrying. "I'm helping her get ready for the barbecue." She giggled. "Uncle Kyle, you just won't believe it when you see how pretty she is!"

"Why wouldn't I believe it? Theresa's always pretty."

"Yes, but now…she looks like a bride!"

The word sent shock waves through him. *Bride* and *Theresa* were not things he'd dared to link in his mind, but the two images together suddenly had a powerful appeal. He took a deep breath, trying to stay calm. *One big decision at a time,* he told himself. *Take care of business first, then worry about the rest.*

He went outside and joined Ken by the barbecue pit, where two briskets were slowly smoking. Some of the neighbors joined them. They commiserated on Kyle's injury and asked about life in Austin. "I heard some political types are raising a big fuss about the goings-on on Sixth Street," one of his high school buddies, Larry Timmons, said. "To hear them talk, it's a regular den of iniquity down there."

"Don't believe everything you hear," he said. "There's nothing illegal or immoral going on. If some folks don't want to see tattoo parlors and lingerie stores, they should stay home or go someplace else."

"I wouldn't mind seeing one of those lingerie stores," a big man named Mike drawled. "Think I could meet one of them Victoria's Secret models if I went shopping there?"

They all laughed, but the laughter faded as one by one their attention shifted toward the house. "Speaking of models," Larry muttered.

"Kyle, is that the girlfriend I heard you brought with you this weekend?" Mike asked as they watched Theresa cross the yard toward them.

"That's her." He swallowed, his heart racing as he watched her pick her way across the grass. She was wearing a white dress with long sleeves and a full skirt trimmed in lace. With her dark hair flowing around her shoulders, she looked like an angel.

She stopped in front of him, smoothing down her skirt, her gaze darting from person to person. "What is everybody staring at?"

He stepped forward and took her hand. "Who wouldn't stare? You look gorgeous."

She tugged down her sleeve. "Do you like it?"

"I do." He caught and held her gaze, wanting her to know the sincerity behind his words. It was something, seeing a woman like her, who could brazenly wear the most provocative outfits, unsure of herself in a soft, sweet dress like this. "You look more beautiful than ever."

"Oh, stop with the mushy stuff. You're embarrassing me." Mike joined them and stuck out his hand. "Hi, I'm Mike Leggit and I've known this fellow since he ate mud pies for lunch and thought girls were icky."

She laughed and took his hand. "Pleased to meet you." She glanced at Kyle. "Did you really eat mud pies?"

"*Once*. And he won't ever let me forget it." He slipped his arm around her waist. "And I never really thought girls were icky, I just pretended to protect my image."

"That's right, Kyle's always fancied himself a ladies' man." Larry shook her hand. "I'm Larry Timmons and I own the ranch next to this one on the east side. We've been trying for years to get Kyle to come home and join the rest of us poor cattle folks, but I can see now he's got better reasons to stay in the city."

"Think you'd like to live on a ranch?" Mike asked.

She glanced at Kyle, then looked away. "I'm afraid I'm a real city girl," she said. "I wouldn't know the first thing about ranching."

"I'll bet you could learn," Mike said. "Kyle could teach you."

"I'm sure Theresa isn't interested in learning about ranching." Kristen must have been standing there listening for a while. When she joined them now, she smiled at Theresa. "That's a gorgeous dress."

"Thank you."

"Howdy, Kristen."

"Hey, Kristen, how are you?"

Once everyone had said hello, the conversation died. Kyle inwardly cringed. Kristen hadn't meant to put a damper on their fun, but that's exactly what she'd done. She was so different from Theresa—so proper and efficient. She was the epitome of what a ranch wife should be—what all their mothers had been. You couldn't joke about lingerie and city girls with the image of your mother standing there, could you?

"We were just telling Kyle how much we missed seeing him around the ranch," Larry said.

"I tell him that all the time." Kristen smiled at him. "I'm sure he'll get tired of Austin and decide to come home one day soon."

"Ranching kind of gets in your blood, I guess," Mike said. "You can't help it, really."

If that's what they all wanted to believe, fine, but that wasn't how Kyle felt. "I like it fine in the city," he said. "I think I'll be settling down there."

Kristen laughed. "That's what he says now, but in a few years he'll be changing his mind."

She talked as though he was still a child who couldn't make up his mind between a red bicycle and a blue one. "No, I won't change my mind," he said firmly.

Her smile faded. "I didn't mean to upset you. We can talk about it later."

"No, I think we'd better talk now." He took Kristen's arm and led her away from the cooker. "Excuse us just a minute, fellows."

"Kyle, what are you doing? I have guests to see to." She tried to pull away from him.

"This won't take a minute. Ken, Theresa, you come, too."

"I don't think…" Theresa took a step back.

"Aw, come on, you might as well hear this, too." Ken took her arm and escorted her across the yard behind Kyle and Kristen.

Kyle stopped in a secluded corner between the kids' sandbox and the fountain Ken had given Kristen for her birthday two years before. Kristen pulled away from him and crossed her arms over her chest. "What has gotten into you?" she asked.

"I've asked Ken to buy out my share of the ranch."

It took a moment for this bombshell to register. Kristen went pale and stared at her husband. "What did you say?"

"I told him I thought it was a good idea." His mouth was set in a grim line. "For everybody."

"I can't believe you agreed to such a crazy idea!" She turned to Kyle. "This ranch is half yours. Daddy left it to both of us in his will."

He shook his head. "It makes no sense for me to own half of something when I'm not here to do any of the work or make any of the decisions. You and Ken are the ones who are doing all the work—you deserve all the reward, too."

"But what will you do with yourself?"

"I'm going to use the money to build a house on my land in Austin, and to start a business."

"Doing what? You don't know how to do anything but ride horses and ranch."

He shifted his weight to one hip. So what if he didn't know anything else? He could learn, couldn't he? "I'm not sure what kind of business yet, but I'm looking into a few things."

She shook her head. "I can't let you make a crazy mistake like this."

All the sympathy he'd been feeling for her fled. "You're not my mother. And I'm not some stupid kid who needs looking after. I can make my own decisions. And if I screw up, then it's my life I'm messing up, not yours."

"How can you say that? I care what happens to you."

"I know." He stared at the ground. Why did she have to make this so hard? If she loved him so much, why couldn't she abide by his decision, wish him well and leave it at that? But then, she wouldn't be his sister if she caved that easily. "I'm going to do this. So make your peace with it."

She glared at him, then charged past them, toward the house. She brushed against Theresa and stepped back. "This is all your fault," she said. "He was never like this before he met you."

Theresa looked stunned as Kristen hurried across the yard in a stiff-legged gait that was almost but not quite at the pace of a run.

"I'm sorry," Kyle said to Theresa. "She shouldn't have said that."

She looked at him, eyes questioning. "You really are selling your half of the ranch?"

He nodded. "I finally figured out it was the only way I could really break the ties, plus get a stake for a fresh start."

"Are you sure you want to do that? I mean…this is your home."

"It's still his home," Ken said. He clapped Kyle on the back. "That hasn't changed. He's welcome here anytime."

Kyle nodded. "This will be best for everybody." He looked toward the house, where Kristen had fled. "I hope she'll see that one day."

"I'll talk to her," Ken said. "It'll be all right."

Ken left them and Kyle turned back to Theresa. "I'd planned to tell you later, after I'd talked it over with Kristen." He looked around at the crowd of people. "Now wasn't exactly the best timing, but I couldn't stand her thinking she could keep planning my future the way she always has."

"I don't know what to think," Theresa said. "I'm a little stunned myself."

"I was hoping you'd be happy for me."

"I am." She nodded. "If this is what you want, then I'm happy."

Then why didn't she look happier? Standing there in that white lacy dress, she looked like a bride who'd been left at the altar.

They needed to talk more, but before he could say so another neighbor, Travis Wiley, grabbed Kyle's arm and insisted he join them for a game of horseshoes. "You can talk to that pretty gal of yours anytime," Old Man Wiley said. "You can only play horseshoes against me once a year."

"You just know you'll whip me because I'm out of practice," he said. "Maybe in a couple of minutes." He turned back to Theresa to continue their conversation, but she was already halfway to the house, her black hair flying like a horse's mane behind her, the full skirt of her white dress billowing out as she hurried across the yard.

THERESA FLUNG OPEN HER suitcase and blindly stuffed clothes into it. She went into the bathroom and swept the counter and the ledge of the tub clean, tossing toothbrush, shampoo and makeup into her travel case. She'd sort everything out when she got home. Right now she just had to get out of here.

When Kyle had faced down his sister and made his announcement, she'd silently cheered, applauding him for refusing to let Kristen bully him. Kyle had looked at her and she'd seen his silent plea for approval. But then Kristen had lashed out at her and she'd panicked.

Was Kristen right? Had Kyle sold away his birthright for *her?* The idea terrified her. It was one thing to imagine that she was in love with Kyle, or even to hope he might love her. But for him to give up so much…and why? Was it really what he wanted? Or only what he thought *she* wanted?

Last night at the creek, they'd been so close. At one point, he'd started to tell her something and she'd immediately brushed him off. She'd been afraid he was going to tell her he loved her, and she wasn't ready for that. Not yet. Maybe not ever.

Had he seen the fear in her eyes and decided that instead of telling her his feelings he'd make some grand gesture to show them to her? He was just the kind of man to do something like that. After all, he'd made a bedroom under the stars and danced almost naked on her coffee table to impress her. Maybe giving up his share of the ranch was the same kind of thing.

She thought of what his friend Mike had said, about ranching being in his blood. If that was true, then turning his back on that for someone else—for a woman with no ties and family of her own—was asking for trouble. What would happen in a few years when he realized he'd made a mistake? Who would he blame his unhappiness on if not her?

She zipped the suitcase shut and glanced around the room, looking for anything she might have left behind. Then she grabbed her purse and the case and tiptoed down the stairs. She stashed the suitcase in the back of Ken's truck, then went to find him.

He was in the kitchen chipping ice, thankfully alone. "Does Wimberley have a bus station?" she asked.

He looked up, startled. "No, you have to go to San Marcos for that."

"Can you take me there? Now? I need to get back to Austin."

He frowned. "Why don't you ask Kyle to take you?"

"I don't want to spoil his fun." She tossed her hair back and tried to look unconcerned. "Something's come up."

Ken laid aside the ice pick and studied her. "You two have a fight or something?"

"No." She twisted her hands together. "Please, will you just take me to the bus station?"

She thought he was going to say no, but after a long silence, he nodded. "Okay, let me get my keys." She followed him out to the truck. "You know you're going to cause all kinds of gossip, don't you?" he said as they climbed in.

"What do you mean?" She fastened her seat belt.

"Everybody'll be talking about how I ran off with my brother-in-law's girlfriend."

"They'll find out the truth when you come back without me."

He grinned. "I don't know. I might just let them think we were up to something. It'll be good for my reputation."

She laughed in spite of the tension coiled in her chest. "You're incorrigible."

"So my wife tells me all the time." He started the engine. "I like to think that's why she married me."

As they pulled away from the house, she stared out the window at the rows of pickup trucks and cars parked under the trees along the drive. "What will you tell Kyle?"

"That you had to leave. That you said something came up. That you wouldn't tell me what it was."

She nodded. Kyle would probably be angry with her, but

maybe that was for the best. If he got mad at her, maybe he'd think more about what he was doing.

"This isn't because he said he is selling his half of the ranch, is it?" Ken asked. "I mean, it's not like it's some big spread worth a lot of money or anything."

She shook her head. "No. It's not about the ranch. It's about me." That at least was the truth. She loved Kyle, but she didn't want him building his future around her. She couldn't handle that kind of responsibility. If you started counting on other people to make you happy, you'd only end up in trouble. Kyle needed to figure that out, and maybe he needed to do it without her.

15

By the time Kyle made it into the house to talk to Theresa, there was no sign of her. When he found the guest bedroom vacant, without so much as a lipstick left behind, he felt as if he'd been kicked in the gut.

He descended the stairs two at a time and barreled into the kitchen, where he found Kristen angrily stabbing toothpicks into jalapeño peppers stuffed with cream cheese. "Where's Theresa?" he demanded.

She impaled another pepper and arranged it on a tray. "How should I know?"

"Her suitcase isn't in her room." He grabbed Kristen's arm and turned her around to face him. "Did you say something else to her? Something to make her want to leave?"

"I didn't say anything to her." She shook loose from him. "If she left, I didn't have anything to do with it."

"Except that you upset her, telling her it was her fault I was selling my share of the ranch. Don't you think I'm man enough to make my own decisions?"

She turned away from him again, shoulders hunched. "Not when it's such a stupid decision."

"It's not stupid." He took a deep breath, struggling to stay calm, to force his way past the blinders she wore, to *make* her understand why he'd done the right thing for all of them. "Look—I know you're my sister, but we aren't twins. We aren't alike. We don't think alike. You love this place and this life, but to me it's always felt like I was trying to wear boots that were too small or a shirt that's too tight." He raked his hand through his hair, struggling to find the right words. "I'm almost thirty years old and I haven't done squat with my life. And you know why? It's because I felt some kind of, I don't know, some kind of *obligation* to keep my hand in here. To try to do what everyone thought I should do— Mom and Dad and you and Ken and all the people we grew up with who looked at me and saw a rancher's son who would be a rancher, too." He shook his head. "But it never felt right to me. I could never make it fit. So I wasted time on the rodeo circuit, thinking if I waited long enough, things would come together for me. But they haven't."

"Maybe you haven't given ranching enough of a chance," she said. "Maybe if you tried—"

He took her hand in his, silencing her. "No. If I was going to make ranching my life, I would have done so by now. And all the waiting in the world isn't going to change anything or get me anywhere."

Twin worry lines stood out on her forehead. "Why now? It seems so sudden. I can't help thinking Theresa had something to do with your decision."

"All Theresa did was show me that there's no crime in living life the way you want to live it—in being yourself and not worrying that that's going to somehow hurt the people who really love you." He squeezed Kristen's hand in his. "You're always saying you want me to be happy.

Well, this is what's going to make me happy. I need this chance to live the kind of life I want to live. I'd like to know you're okay with that, but even if you're not, this is something I have to do."

He saw the struggle reflected in Kristen's eyes as she weighed this ultimatum. She studied him for a long moment, as if searching for some confirmation that this wasn't another of his phases, that he was serious this time. At last she nodded, though her voice still held doubt. "If you're sure…"

"I'm sure."

She slipped her hand from his and straightened her shoulders. "What about Theresa? Where does she fit into all this?"

"I'm not sure. I guess that depends on her." He took a deep breath, trying to control the sudden alarming shakiness in his voice. "I thought when I first met her she'd just be a way to pass the time while I was recovering—a phase, like you said. But she's turned out to mean a lot more to me than that. I—I love her and I hope she feels the same way about me." Saying the words out loud made his heart pound and he folded his arms over his chest, as if he could keep in the combination of fear and giddiness rocketing around inside of him.

Kristen's expression softened. "Oh, Kyle. I had no idea…."

He gave one sharp bark of laughter. "It's wild, isn't it?" He looked around the kitchen. "And now she's gone haring off who knows where. What am I going to do?"

She came and put her arm around him. "You'll go find her and you'll grovel if you have to." She smiled. "Women appreciate that sometimes, you know."

"But what if she doesn't want anything to do with me?"

"Don't borrow trouble." She pushed him away. "Go on now. Go find her. You'll be all right. I promise."

"That's what you always say. Like you know everything."

"Sometimes I do." She smiled. "For instance, I know I haven't given you enough credit before now." She turned back to the tray of peppers. "I'm going to try to change that, but old habits die hard."

"If I can change, you can, too. And I hope Theresa can change a little, too, and let me into her life on a more permanent basis."

"Go. Don't waste any more time."

"That's true. I've wasted enough already." He kissed her cheek. "Thanks."

"But I didn't do anything."

"You listened. And you understood. That's a lot in my book."

"Go!"

THERESA TOOK A CAB FROM THE bus station to Austin Body Art. When she walked in, Cherry and Scott looked up from where they'd had their heads together over the computer, startled. "Theresa! What are you doing here?" Cherry asked.

"Let's just say the weekend didn't turn out to be as relaxing as I'd hoped." She stuffed her purse and suitcase behind the counter.

"Oh, no! Did something happen with Kyle?" Cherry asked. "Did you two have a fight?"

Maybe it would have been better if they'd had a real knock-down, drag-out battle. Instead they'd left too many things unsaid. "I don't want to talk about it."

"Oh." Cherry clearly was disappointed not to be getting the inside scoop. Then she brightened. "That's a great dress."

"Yeah," Scott agreed. "I've never seen you in a dress before."

"What's that supposed to mean?" In all the turmoil, she'd forgotten all about what she was wearing. Now she'd never hear the end of it. *The tiger lady changed her leather and denim for a white lace dress? Who does she think she is?* She straightened her shoulders and glared at him. "I can wear a dress if I want to."

He took a step back. "You can wear anything you want. I just meant you look nice, that's all."

"You do look really nice," Cherry said. "White is a great color with your dark hair. That fitted bodice is really flattering, too." She nodded. "You should wear dresses more often."

Just what she needed—fashion advice from a girl whose entire wardrobe looked as if it had been purchased at a rummage sale put on by Gypsies.

She flipped open the appointment book and scowled at it. "What's been going on here while I was gone?"

"Nothing too exciting." Scott looked over her shoulder. "It hasn't been busy, but it's been fairly steady. And hey, we got these." He picked up a stack of bumper stickers from beside the cash register and handed them to her. "Madeline brought them by yesterday."

Save Sixth Street! the bumper sticker proclaimed.

"The business owners' coalition has been busy," Cherry said. "They held a big press conference and rally yesterday and hope to get some good coverage. They're trying to show that Sixth Street isn't as sleazy as 'Clean' Carter and his bunch have made out."

"Hmph. Good luck with that. I just hope it's not too late. The election is only a couple of weeks away."

"I think that's enough time," Cherry said.

"Maybe." Even if the coalition succeeded in defeating Carter and bringing business back to the area, she wasn't sure she wanted to stay here anymore. Maybe she'd let Scott run the shop while she visited Zach in Chicago. She might even decide to stay in the Windy City, or she could go to New Orleans or even New York. She'd spent her whole life in Austin; maybe it was time she saw more of the world. After all, she didn't have anything or anyone to hold her here. The thought made her stomach hurt.

"I designed a new tat," Scott said. "Want to see?"

"Sure." Anything to avoid more talk about her own screwed-up situation. She summoned a look of interest.

He flipped open a sketchbook and showed her a drawing of a tree branch and a star. "Is that a pecan tree?" she asked.

He grinned. "Exactly."

"Why? Because you're nuts?"

He made a face at her. "No, it's because before they switched to numbering streets, this was Pecan Street."

"And the star is for Austin, the capital," Cherry added.

"Very nice." Theresa nodded. "Where are you going to put it?"

He pointed to his forearm. "Right here. I want to be able to see it all the time."

She glanced at the appointment book again. "There's no one scheduled. I can do it for you right now." Nothing like work to take her mind off her personal problems.

"You can't do that!" Cherry put out her hand as if to physically stop her. "You'll ruin that gorgeous dress."

Theresa glanced down at the dress. "It doesn't matter. I don't plan to ever wear it again." Too many bad memories were tied up in this dress.

"It's still too beautiful to ruin."

"Besides, I kind of wanted Cherry to ink this one." Scott flushed as he cast a sideways look at his co-worker. "I mean, she and I came up with this together."

"That's right." Cherry picked up a pen from the counter, then set it back down. "I mean, we weren't expecting you back or anything." The tips of the girl's ears were as red as her hair.

Some of the fog lifted from Theresa's brain. All the shared glances, the physical closeness and the conspiratorial smiles suddenly made sense. She looked at the two more closely. "I thought you two didn't like each other."

"Why would you think that?" It was Cherry's turn to look defensive.

Scott coughed. "We didn't know each other very well, that's all."

Cherry glanced at him. "Once I figured out the whole playboy thing was just an act, I discovered he wasn't so bad after all."

"Just an act?" Theresa gave him a skeptical look. "All those different women? All the parties?"

He flushed. "Maybe I exaggerated a little bit."

"Uh-huh." She bet there was a hell of a story behind that little confession, but she was too weary to pursue it at the moment.

"So, uh, is it okay if Cherry does this tattoo?"

"Sure. Cherry can do it. I was just offering."

"You look worn out," Cherry said. "Why don't you go on home and get some rest? We can take care of things here."

Scott nodded. "Yeah. We'll hold down the fort while you get some rest."

They both looked at her as though they expected her to keel over at any moment. "When did I turn into an old lady who has to go home and take a nap in the middle of the afternoon?" Besides, the last thing she wanted right now was to be alone. Once there was no one else around to distract her, she was sure her own thoughts would close in and she'd start doubting her decision to run away from Kyle.

Cherry gave her a funny look. "I didn't say you were old—you just seem a little upset."

"I am not upset!" She cringed when she heard the shrillness of her voice. Okay, she needed to get a grip here. She took a deep breath. "I'll be fine. And I don't want to go home. I'll just…go over the accounts or something." Sure. Nothing like a little number crunching to depress her even further. Then again, no sense saving the task for later and risking spoiling a good mood. If she was going to wallow in misery, might as well go whole-hog.

THE FIRST THING KYLE SAW when he reached downtown Austin was a banner stretched over Lamar announcing Save Sixth Street! *About time somebody gave Carter a dose of his own medicine,* he thought as he turned onto East Sixth. Now if he could just make Theresa listen to reason….

When he walked into Austin Body Art, he saw that he'd guessed right—she'd come here rather than to her apartment. She was frowning at the computer screen, looking a little out of place against the backdrop of colorful flashes in that white, lacy dress. Seeing that dress reminded him that there was a soft, romantic woman beneath her tough-girl disguise. The idea gave him hope. The romantic woman was the one he needed to reach right now.

"Theresa?"

She looked up from the computer, and the flash of pain in her eyes wounded him. But then she covered it up with a hard look. She pushed her chair back from the computer and stood. "What are you doing here?"

He walked over and stood at the counter. "I could ask you the same thing. Last I checked, you were supposed to be at a barbecue at my sister's house. Why did you run out of there that way?"

The lines around her mouth tightened. "Kristen's right. I don't belong with that crowd."

"Who says? My friends liked meeting you. They were asking about you."

She looked away from him. "I didn't see any point in hanging around any longer," she mumbled.

"Oh, you didn't? You didn't think there were a few things you and I needed to talk about?"

She glanced toward the tattoo chair where Cherry was inking a design on Scott, the two of them trying to pretend they weren't listening to every word that was said. She looked at Kyle again. "I don't know what to say to you."

He leaned on the counter, tempted to reach out and touch her. Maybe some physical contact would make her realize the connection they had. "Tell me the real reason you ran away."

She looked down at the floor. "You scared me," she said softly, the words clearly a struggle.

"Scared you?" He blinked, confused. "What did I do to scare you?"

Her eyes met his again, her confusion evident. "You said you were giving up your share of the ranch. Why would you do that all of a sudden—give up your home that way?"

He frowned. "I thought you of all people understood that. The ranch is my home, but it's not my future. I realized it was time to let go of it and get on with my life."

She gripped the edge of the counter. "And this had nothing to do with me?"

He moved around the counter to stand in front of her. He couldn't stand having that barrier between them any more than he could bear this misunderstanding dividing them. "It had a lot to do with you, actually."

If he'd expected her to be happy about that news, he'd been wrong. She went pale and her eyes took on a shiny look, as if she was on the verge of tears. "Dammit, what did I say now?" he asked. "That was supposed to be good news."

She shook her head. "I don't want you changing your life because of me." Her eyes met his, her expression desperate. "I don't want that kind of responsibility. Later on, when you realize you've made a mistake, you'll hate me for it."

"Who says I've made a mistake?" Anger pinched at him, but he pushed it away. "Look, I said you had a lot to do with my decision, but I didn't do this for you. I did it for me."

"Then what do I have to do with it?"

Standing here looking at her wasn't enough anymore. He grabbed her hand, holding on. He didn't want her running out on him again—ever. "You are one of the strongest people I know." He rubbed his thumb across her knuckles, feeling the fine bones and the softness of her skin. Amazing how such delicacy could conceal such strength. And how her toughness was a front for such a vulnerable spirit. "Life dealt you a tough hand, but you've made the best of it," he continued. "You do your own thing and you don't let other people try to tell you how to live. I watched you and learned that I could do that, too—and I didn't have to be afraid of losing the people I love in the process."

He squeezed her hand and she raised her eyes to meet his. The yearning he saw there matched the feelings he'd been fighting for days now. He kissed her palm and flashed a brief smile. "You made me think, which can be a dangerous thing sometimes, but there you have it. All that thinking helped me figure out what I want to do with my life."

She wet her lips. "And what is it you want to do?"

"I can do better than just tell you. I can show you."

He tugged her toward the door, the bells jangling wildly as he led her outside. Excitement made him hurry until he was half dragging her down the sidewalk after him. He stopped in front of the front window of the Waterloo Tavern. "Take a good look," he said.

She stared at the bar, puzzled. "What am I looking at, exactly?"

"I've decided to buy and run the Waterloo Tavern." He grinned at the building, already imagining the changes he'd make: new awnings, fresh paint on the sign, more advertising to draw the crowds....

"You're going to own a bar?" She shook her head. "I'm still trying to figure out the connection."

"Think about it and you'll see it's perfect. I don't like getting up early and I don't mind staying up late, so the hours are perfect. I'll be right here in the heart of the city, not stuck out in the country. The money I'll get from selling my half of the ranch will give me a good down payment on the bar and leave enough to make a start on my dream house on that land I showed you."

She nodded. "But what if business doesn't pick up on Sixth Street? You could lose everything."

"Are you always such a pessimist?" He put his arm around her. "Listen, when times are bad, what do people do? They drink. And when they're good, they drink, too. So I figure a bar is one of the safer bets around. Not to mention I think this whole 'Clean' Carter campaign is going to backfire on the esteemed council member. This is Austin, Texas, after all. Home to university students, hippies, slackers, politicians, environmentalists and urban cowboys. And every one of those groups likes to party with the best of them. Carter and his bunch don't stand a chance."

She nodded. "You have a point. And the business owners are fighting back now. That will help."

"Exactly. So what do you think of my plan?"

She nodded. "It makes sense."

He'd hoped for a little more enthusiasm. Then again, she'd spent her whole life building up her armor, trying to keep from getting hurt. It would take more than subtle hints to get through to her. "Think you can stand having me right next door?" he asked.

He was rewarded with a small smile. "I think I can stand it."

Okay, time to bring in the big guns. He hoped he wasn't

making a mistake here, but he'd promised himself he was through being slow and cautious. That never got a man anywhere in the rodeo arena or in life. Sucking in a deep breath, he dropped to one knee on the sidewalk in front of her.

The stunned look on her face was almost worth making a fool of himself this way. "Wh-what are you doing?" she stammered.

He took both of her hands in his. "The first day I met you, Theresa Jacobs, I knew you were a special woman." He cleared his throat, trying to keep it together long enough to get out the speech he'd rehearsed. "You've taught me things and made me feel things that no other woman could have done. And you made me fall in love with you."

She gasped and tried to pull away, but he held her fast. The rush of tenderness in her eyes kept him from panicking. "I love you, too," she whispered, blinking fast, her lashes glistening with tears she was fighting back.

He squeezed her hands and shifted a little on the sidewalk, trying to ignore the pebble lodged beneath his knee. He had to get through this. "I love you enough that I want you to be a part of my starting over. In fact, I'm not sure I can do it without you to remind me what stubborn really is."

She let out a choked laugh. "Is that supposed to be a compliment?"

"You could take it that way." He grinned. "I had a lot of other fancy words to say, but it's getting uncomfortable down here, so I'll skip to the main question—Will you marry me?"

She swayed a little, and he wondered if he was going to have to catch her. He hadn't figured her for the swooning type, but what did he know about women, anyway?

Luckily she regained her balance, if not her composure. "Marry? Kyle, I—" She shook her head. "I don't know what to say."

"Do you love me?"

"Yes! Yes, I do." She smiled. "It's crazy, but I really do."

"Then say yes."

"It's such a big step. What if it doesn't—"

He stood and gathered her into his arms, silencing her with a kiss. "We'll be good together," he said softly, brushing the hair back from her forehead. "You don't have to be afraid. I'm never going to do anything to hurt you."

"Promise?" She smiled.

"I promise."

She nodded. "Then yes. Yes, I'll marry you." She covered her mouth with her hand. "I can't believe I said that."

"It took you long enough," he teased.

She looked at him through half-lowered lashes. "You're in trouble now, cowboy. Don't you know I'm stubborn and outspoken and opinionated and known to be a little wild?"

"All the things I like about you most." He lowered his mouth to hers, thinking as he did so of all the kisses they'd share in the years to come. This was the feeling he'd been searching for his whole life—this sense that he was exactly where he was supposed to be, doing exactly what he was supposed to be doing, with the person he was supposed to be doing it with.

It felt as though he'd come home. At last.

"Kyle?"

"Hmm?"

"What is that man doing across the street?"

He looked up and spotted the lanky figure with a camera. The photographer smiled and waved. "I think he's taking our picture."

"Oh. I think he might be a reporter."

"Then we'd better give him something good to photograph." He pulled her closer and kissed her again, bending her over backward in an extravagant, romantic gesture. He didn't intend to do anything halfway ever again, and that included loving his impossible, stubborn, sexy, incredible wife.

Epilogue

"DID YOU SEE THE NEWS?" A little over two weeks later, Kyle burst into Austin Body Art waving the paper in front of him.

Theresa looked up from the tattoo she was inking and shut off the tattoo machine. "Madeline was in here a few minutes ago to tell us 'Clean' Carter lost."

"They really slammed him." He waved the paper at her. "I knew the voters would come to their senses."

"I think it was that picture of you two that turned the tide." Cherry looked up from tuning her cello.

"You mean the one of us kissing?" He grinned.

"Maybe she means our engagement announcement photo." Theresa couldn't resist teasing him. After all, it was the exact same shot. The photographer had used some kind of filter to blur the edges of the image so that he'd captured the two of them in that incredibly romantic embrace. It reminded her of the shot she'd seen of a soldier kissing a nurse on the streets of New York at the end of World War II.

"I saw that picture," her customer said. He studied Theresa more closely. "I didn't even recognize you at first. You looked like a bride in that white dress."

"Exactly," Cherry said. "After that photo ran on the

front page of the Austin paper, Sixth Street's image went from sleazy to romantic in one afternoon. Suddenly everyone wanted to come ride in one of the horse-drawn carriages, go slow dancing at the clubs and share dessert and coffee and gaze soulfully at each other in one of the cafés." She rolled her eyes and drew her bow across the cello, playing a long note.

"And don't forget tattoos," Scott said. "We advertised a couples special and had all the business we could handle doing matching tats for people."

"Yeah, it was a cool idea." Cherry stretched out her ankle to admire the pecan tree and lone star there, a match for the one on Scott's forearm. "But it doesn't feel so special anymore," she teased.

"I'll show you special." He bent and began kissing her neck, while she squealed.

"Children, calm down," Theresa ordered with mock fierceness. She turned her attention back to Kyle. "How's the remodeling going today?"

"It's going good. But I'm sure glad we were able to do a quick closing on the deal. There's a lot of work to do."

"Are you sure we'll be ready by next month? Maybe we should set another date...." They'd decided to hold their wedding reception at the tavern as a combination marriage and grand-opening celebration.

"No way," Kyle said. "It'll be done, even if I have to recruit everyone I know to help." He came over and kissed her cheek. "Besides, I don't want to give you time to change your mind."

She shook her head. "I'm not going to change my mind." Zach had teased her about her haste to get to the altar after she'd refused all thoughts of marriage for so many years. She'd told him she had a lot of lost time to make up for. Besides, wasn't June the perfect time for a wedding?

"I'd better get back to work," he said. "Stop by later and check out the progress." He winked and she felt the same warm, syrupy feeling in her stomach she always felt when he looked at her these days. Who'd have thought being in love would do so much for a person's outlook on life?

"Remind me later to show you the decorations Kristen sent over," he added.

She made a face. "Let me guess—hearts and doves and those white crepe bells."

"Of course." He laughed. "We have an image to live up to, you know."

"Zach's never going to let me live this down."

"When are he and Jen coming down?"

"In two weeks. His semester's over and she has a break from the show, so they'll be able to stay until the wedding."

"If he's anything like you, I'm going to be in trouble."

"What's that supposed to mean?"

"One stubborn person in the family is enough, thank you very much."

"Who are you calling stubborn, Mr. I Won't Take No For An Answer?" She grinned.

"Good thing, too." He bent and kissed her cheek. "See you tonight?"

"Maybe." She slid her mouth close to his ear. "Wear your chaps?"

"I was thinking of saving them for the honeymoon."

"No, you won't need them on the honeymoon."

"I won't?"

She shook her head. "In fact, if I were you, I wouldn't bother packing a suitcase. We won't be going out."

He grinned. "Is that so?"

She nodded. A week with her new husband naked seemed as good a way as any to start off a marriage.

He rubbed his hands together and backed toward the door. "In that case, I'd better save my strength. And I think I have to work tonight."

She smiled and switched the tattoo machine back on. He'd said the same thing every night for the past week, but he'd always shown up at her place just the same. She was counting on the fact that he'd always be there. The idea was scary and amazing and downright wonderful.

Exactly like falling in love.

Who knew?

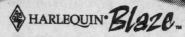

If you enjoyed what you just read,
then we've got an offer you can't resist!

Take 2 bestselling love stories FREE!

Plus get a FREE surprise gift!

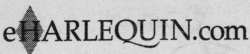

Enjoy the launch of Maureen Child's
NEW miniseries

THREE-WAY WAGER

*The Reilly triplets bet they could go
ninety days without sex. Hmmm.*

The Tempting Mrs. Reilly
by MAUREEN CHILD

(Silhouette Desire #1652)
Available May 2005

Brian Reilly had just made a bet to not
have sex for three months when his
stunningly sexy ex-wife blew into town.
It wasn't long before Tina had him
contemplating giving up his wager
and getting her back. But the tempting
Mrs. Reilly had a reason of her own
for wanting Brian to lose his bet…
to give her a baby!

HARLEQUIN® Blaze™

Three daring sisters put their lives—
and their hearts—on the line in

Cara Summer's

thrilling new mini-series.

Risking It All

Don't miss:

THE PROPOSITION
May 2005

THE DARE
June 2005

THE FAVOR
July 2005

Don't miss the adventure!

Available wherever Harlequin books are sold.